TALL IN THE SADDLE

BY STEVE J. JOHNSON

DEDICATED to all who live the honest cowboy way of life,
where one's word means what it says,
and a simple handshake binds a contract.

Tall in the Saddle
First Edition. Text and Illustrations Copyright © 2015, 2017 by Steve J. Johnson
All rights reserved. No part of this work may be reproduced by any means whatsoever,
either mechanical, digital or electronic, except for brief portions quoted for review.

Editors: Jenny Songer Harris, Stephanie Clayburn and David Toone

Special thanks to Perpetua Printing, LLC, whose financial assistance and guidance
helped make the publication of this book possible.

Printed in the United States of America

Library of Congress Cataloging-in-Publication Data
   Johnson, Steve J., 1963
   Tall in the Saddle / story and illustrations by Steve J. Johnson.
   Summary: A coming of age story centered on a boy named Cooper. How he and his
   family live a contemporary cowboy lifestyle and thrive.
   ISBN 978-1-944141-20-2
   (1. Biography – Non Fiction)

CONTENTS

THE COW JUMPED OVER THE MOON

Hey diddle, diddle
The boy took a piddle,
And the cow jumped over the moon.

The little dog laughed to see such a sight
When it happens again,
It will surely be too soon.

A boy doing his business
In all of his glory
Is just the antic to set the stage
For this fun-loving story.

PROLOGUE

The ringing of the phone broke the midmorning silence of an everyday routine inside a house once filled with the ruckus of four rambunctious siblings.

"Hello, how can I help you?"

"Hey Pops, what's up?" came the upbeat voice from the other end of the line.

"Well, I'm not sure but I have a feelin' you're gonna let me know," Pops said.

"Actually, Dad, I was wonderin' if you could find a way to meet me Friday afternoon with a horse trailer down by the freeway at the truck stop?"

"I'm sure I can. What have you got goin'?" Pops mumbled to himself, "That boy is always flyin' by the seat of his pants."

"What did you say, Pops?"

"Ah, nothin'. Just tell me what you've got up your sleeve, Coop."

"Well, Jack is passin' through and he'll have two horses that I need to take with me, so I was wonderin' if you could bring a trailer and meet us there to take the horses home until I can get there?"

"Hang on, hold your horses, Coop. Tell me what's happenin'?" Pops said as his thoughts were trying to catch up with the conversation. Cooper had been away to his first year of college which was winding down, but apparently something else was ramping up.

Without hesitation, Cooper plowed ahead, "Oh yeah, I forgot to tell you. It's a long story but I think you're gonna like it. I've been takin' these equine classes here at college and heard of some ranch internship opportunities that are offered to students. One of the internships is on a cattle ranch in Wyoming, so I applied and I got it! Pretty cool, huh?"

"You got the job? Good for you! When do you start?"

"I have to be there by the first of May. I'm sure lookin' forward to goin' back to Wyoming for the summer and they're even talkin' about sendin' me out to Nebraska to cowboy on another one of their outfits later on. They told me to bring three horses. I knew you needed yours at home, so I called around to see if I could find some others. Jack is gonna pay me to ride a couple of colts for him all summer, so I can make double money."

"Well it sounds like you've got it all figured out. That's a pretty good deal. Good for you," Pops conceded.

After the arrangements to meet and pick up the horses were made, goodbyes were said and silence once more filled the old homestead.

Pops wasn't old by any means, but he did move a little more deliberately and he also thought twice when climbing on a green colt, so keeping up with his "on the move" kids took some doing.

"That boy sure is busy and he's real good at draggin' me into his crazy schemes," Pops muttered to himself, reflecting on how this all began, where the time had gone, and the twists and turns of life over the past twenty years that had led to this point. A flood of memories washed over him.

Pops sat back in his rocking chair, folded his arms, gazed out the window, and considered his youngest son. A wise feller once said, "The best way to live twice as long as the next guy is to just live twice as much in the same amount of time."

Come share this crazy fun-filled adventure,
Hang tight for the ride where e're it goes.
Over peaks, through valley and pastures,
From deserts to belly-deep snows.

Hear the squeak of well-worn saddles,
Cherish good times for kids of all ages.
Peek into the past and glimpse the future,
Stir memories with the turn of these pages.

"Stud"

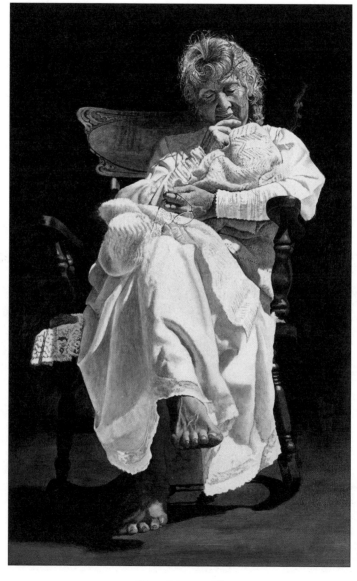

"Grand Approval"

1. BIRTHDAY SURPRISE

This crazy adventure called "Cooper" began some twenty years before. January 27, 1994, brought the birth of the fourth and final child born to Pops and Momma K. After some conversation within the family and a little thinking, his name was decided—Cooper.

For the most part, he came into the world the usual way, amid the typical excitement of any addition to a family. As Pops held the small, squirming bundle that smelled of fresh linens and the unmistakable scent of newborn baby, he was standing next to the bed where this new little boy's proud mother lay. His three excited siblings were jumping about and pleading, "Can I hode him? Pwease?" Pops looked at them and back at the new babe as he considered what the future would hold for this little feller. "We won't dwop him," the siblings all promised earnestly.

"Alright, you can hode him but you must be sitting down so you don't dwop him," Pops reluctantly consented.

When Annie, Cooper's one and only sister, first learned that Momma K was expecting another boy, she was momentarily heartbroken. She sobbed, "Mommy, but I wanted a sistew." She offered a solution, "When you get the baby bwudder out of your tummy can you just put a witto baby sistew in dere?"

Momma K thought out loud, "We'll see what we can do."

Pops, overhearing the exchange, said to Momma K, "Don't listen to that little girl. She's tired and doesn't know what she's talkin' about."

Annie had since reconciled her concerns about having another brother and now she was the most insistent. "Can I sit up on the bed by Mommy and hode my baby bwudder furst?" In her innocence and her little girl drive, she naturally took charge.

"You bet, climb up on the bed by Mommy." Annie quickly scrambled into place and Pops laid the red-faced boy in her waiting arms. She looked at him with pride and beamed as she sat beside her happy, yet exhausted mother.

Pops couldn't recall too many details about that blessed day other than "It was a cold day in January," as they say. But one aspect of the day cannot be forgotten, he is reminded regularly. As Momma K lay there in the hospital bed with all the kids huddled around her, she whispered "Happy Birthday." Of course it's a happy birthday, Pops thought. The questioning look on his face prompted her next statement, "How do you like your birthday present?" In the excitement of the commotion that goes along with the birth of a child, Pops had totally forgotten that this day was his birthday also. What a present! That day truly marked the starting point of a bond and the beginning of Cooper's part in the family's story.

"Can we take him home?" One of the kids asked, "And keep him, too?"

This was a joyous occasion, but Pops allowed other things to be on his mind. When the kids said "Take him home," he thought to himself, Yes I would love to take him home, but he regretted taking this little feller back to where they lived. At the time of Cooper's birth, the family was living in a basement apartment in the city, and had been for a few years. This was definitely not Pop's idea of "livin' the dream."

When Pops and Momma K were first married and until the first two kids came along, they lived out in the country in a small town where they owned and operated a modest horse training facility. Pops also did paintings and drawings of cowboys and other jobs to make ends meet, but money was always short. In an effort to conform to and follow the lead

"Momma's Pride"

of educated society, they bit the bullet so to speak. With a couple of kids in tow, they traded it all in to go back to college and finish a degree in hopes of a more promising future for the growing family.

With college recently finished, Pops was working at what he called a transitional job (You know—not the dream job—just something to put food on the table.) He had been in the basement long enough, and he was itching to get out of the city. He wanted to put these kids in what he thought was the proper environment for kids to be raised. (Of course he was only thinking of the children…)

They had previously put some money down on a place in the same small town where they had first lived. The property was a little more than four acres and had a few falling down outbuildings. There was also an unlivable, dilapidated adobe brick farmhouse originally built in 1905. Even though they technically had a place, they still had nowhere to live.

Knowing Pops' feelings and having a healthy drive of her own, over the next few months Momma K got busy on a secret plan.

"What time will you be home?" Momma K asked as Pops was leaving for work one morning.

"The usual time—five or six—dependin' on how things go."

"We'll be looking for you," she said through a sly grin.

Pops didn't think much of it, "See you all later," he said as he waved good bye.

During the day his phone rang. "We're goin' up to the old house today. I just want to let the kids run and play. You know just get away from here for a while and let them get dirty and have some fun. Why don't you meet us there after work?" Momma K said from the other end of the phone line.

"That sounds good. I'll get away as soon as I can. Have some fun for me until I get there."

Pops left as early as he could and went to meet them. As he drove into the yard, something was sure enough different. Things seemed a little fishy. Alongside the old house was a small camp trailer. As Pops got closer, he could tell that it was hooked up to the old water hydrant and plugged into a makeshift electrical set up. It had the look of being parked there for keeps. Pops cautiously got out of the car and strolled over to check it out.

"Surprise! Welcome home!" The whole crew jumped out from behind the trailer and ambushed him with hugs. "Do you like our new house?" They were anxious for his response.

Ol' Pops was surprised all right. He wasn't sure what to say but he was all in. For the next year and a half, they all worked together to remodel the old house, just to make it livable. Pops said many times that, "A smart person would have just torn the old shack down and built a new one." But, according to Momma K, they remodeled it with love and that's what counts.

In the meantime, they were like sardines in a flat tin can. All six of them were packed into a twenty-three foot camp trailer. They weren't pretending to camp. It was for real, yet it was for good. Every chance they'd get, the whole family slept out under the stars. They built cooking fires most every day which made for many evenings of hot chocolate and cherished memories. One of the kids' favorite things to do was cook pancakes on a flat rock heated in the center of the fire. With four acres, the family's "horse life" was slowly coming back. They were again sort of "livin' the dream."

"Can we go to the river and play?" the kids would often ask.

"I'll come along and bring a blanket for us to sit on. We have to be careful and watch out for Cooper. He's not very big you know," Momma K would say. The kids would add "We're gonna build a hut," or "We're goin' fishin'." Now that's how kids, of all ages, should spend their time, Pops thought.

One quiet moment in the trailer as they watched the kids play in the yard, Momma K whispered to Pops, "Even though we are cramped up in this little camp trailer, I feel like I've died and gone to heaven."

Pops added, remembering his recent escape from the city, "Yeah and I feel like I've been to hell and back."

As Cooper grew he was a typical young boy, for the most part. He was brimming with an endless imagination, colorful and daring, but his tender green eyes and raggedy, soft blonde hair peeking from under a wide-brimmed hat hinted at his very tender side. Curiosity, ambition, and sparkly-eyed mischief were all packed into one little feller courageous enough to want to be a cowboy. To know Cooper was to love him, but to understand Cooper one must know a little about his siblings.

Levi was the oldest brother, and he assumed the natural tendencies that go along with that station. He was steady, a sure enough buddy, stubbornly protective, and a real rough-and-tumble cowboy. He had curly hair, a contagious smile, and a chuckly little laugh. Once when he was quite young, one of the other kids was drawing a colorful crayon picture of a horse and Levi protested, "That's not right. Horses are brown!" And he was not budging. From that point on he received the affectionate Indian nickname of "Chief Brown Horse."

Isaac, just a year younger than Levi, was a real mustang. He had feathery blonde hair that he liked cut short. He was wiry and speedy, always in a race, his little cowboy boots clickety-clacking across the ground as he sped along. His little elbows were always flapping as if he were riding a galloping horse. He wore his black felt hat pulled down so tight on his head that his ears were pushed out flat. He had darting eyes, a smirkish grin, and a heart as soft as pudding. He was all about making things fun.

Cheyenne, the golden-haired sister nicknamed Annie, could melt any heart with her adorable smile and cheerful, straightforward self. She was ever attentive and always concerned for "her boys" and their well-being. She was never left out and always had her fingers on the pulse of cowgirl fashion. She was regularly duded up just like her brothers, and she would hit the trail with her pearl-handled cap guns blazing. The infamous Annie Oakley had nothing on her.

After a long day of working on the house, it was time for supper. Momma K took good care of her seemingly always hungry family. Afterward, the table was cleared and the dishes were cleaned up, then the beds in the small trailer would be put together and made up. The tired and fed crew would all get snuggled in for the night. As they lay cuddled together, it never failed that one of the sleepy kipper snacks would ask something like, "Pops, did you have a pony when you were little?"

The bedtime tales would begin. "No, my dad didn't have much use for ponies. He made sure we just had big horses to ride."

"Did Grandpa Eddy have a pony when he was little?" another prodded.

Grandpa Eddy, 1946

"I guess he did of sorts. When I was little like you, he told me many stories about a little grey mustang that he rode everywhere when he was a kid. I think he called the pony Smokey."

"Tell us all about Smokey," they'd say.

"Now it's time to go to sleep so let's wind it down." Pops said as if he was all given out and not interested in telling stories.

Levi chimed in, "Didn't you tell us before that Grandpa Eddy had great big horses?"

"Yes I did. He and his father and his father before him lived up in Idaho. They farmed lots of ground, grew spuds, and harvested meadow hay along the banks of the meandering Snake River. Now that's a big river. And they did it all with big draft horse teams, mostly of the Percheron and Belgium types. My dad would ride on those big horses and when it was time for stackin' hay, he would spend all day ridin' the derek horse."

Great granddad Anthon, 1918

Now Pops was on a roll. The story pump was primed and all the kids had to do was pump it a little from time to time to keep it flowing.

"What's a derek horse again?" Isaac pumped.

"A derek is a big timber contraption rigged with pulleys and ropes. It sort of looks like a modern construction crane and it was used to pile loose hay into large stacks so they could store it. Then they'd feed it to the cattle when winter time came and the derek horse or a team of derek horses, is what powered it and lifted the hay," Pops explained.

Cooper, along with the other kids, listened intently to those tales. Like seeds for the future, they seemed to plant themselves in Coop's little heart. Later on, at one time or another, similar experiences would take root and eventually blossom in his life. Most of the stories Pops told were about their ancestors, where they lived, and how they lived their lives, mostly from the back of a horse.

Pops would go on to say, "Back when I was a little feller . . ." and he'd reminisce while offering wisdom from the past. "You know Grandpa Eddy would tell me things like, 'What's good for the outside of a horse is good for the inside of a man.' Grandpa Eddy's was a good life, one that depended on real horsepower, the kind that was needed every day. It was used to dig up the earth, plant the seeds of the day, and turn over another tomorrow again and again. It was an honest way of livin.'" Pops felt it was the real way of life.

Through sleepy eyes, Coop asked, "Where are the Grandpas now?"

Pops quietly whispered, "Well Coop, they're somewhere out there and they're ridin' horses. I'm sure they're ridin' tall in the saddle. They're on a new outfit now. They cover the range for the Big Ranch."

"The Big Ranch?" Coop queried.

"You know the one way up in the sky, where the grass is always green and stirrup high, where the rivers flow clear, and the range stretches from horizon to horizon, and never a fence in sight," Pops described.

That may not have answered his question, but Coop was satisfied to believe that the grandfathers were still riding tall somewhere. Through those stories about his grandpas and their love of ponies and horses, the emotions were able to cross time and generations to be ingrained deeply in Cooper. He was bound to become a real buckaroo. He constantly dreamed that one day he would have a pony of his very own. Someday just you wait and see, his unspoken determination always seemed to say.

Although these four children had the usual sibling skirmishes and rivalries, for the most part their growing up years were about running faster, jumping higher, building campfires, and playing hide-and-go-seek and horseback-tag in the tall canary grass of the river bottoms near their soon- to-be-fixed-up home.

Once the stories died down and the trailer grew quiet, all the little sardines would drift off to sleep and continue to dream.

"Momma's Shadow"

"Tenderness"

2. LOVE OF LITTLE ANIMALS

A few adventurous years had gone by when Cooper and his brothers, along with two neighbor boys, Spud and Shawn, were playing on the bank of the creek directly behind the old house. At least, Pops and Momma K assumed the boys were on the creek bank. The creek was swollen with the spring runoff from the melting mountain snow. It wasn't a rushing rapid, but a rather bulging slow-moving inlet to the lake not far from the house.

It was early April, the season when winter is mostly gone but summer is not yet ready to fully show itself. The air was still quite cool even with the sun shining high in the sky. The boys were wading through the grasses on the edge of the flooded stream looking for whatever excitement that might pop up. "Hey look at this!" or "Guys! Look at that, did you see that?" one would shout as a fish would go zooming by or some other noteworthy discovery was made. Water, mud, kids, time, invention … those are the things real fun is made of. Just a few days before, most of this water had lived in a snow bank on the nearby mountainside and now it was not much warmer than liquid snow.

Like boy scouts, these kids were "prepared." Well, sort of prepared. They had covered their insulated snow boots with plastic garbage bags, secured with duct tape and twine string. It was an ambitious attempt to make fishing waders—true redneck engineering to make any parent proud. The modified boots were bulky and the grass was wet and thick. There were all sorts of driftwood pieces floating on the water's surface that poked at the "waders" and tore small holes, causing them to slowly leak. The boys, unconcerned, were sloshing about having a great time as they floundered in the floodwater.

A few early migratory birds were flying overhead and some were taking a break floating on the river's surface, enjoying the sparkling sunshine as the water lapped softly against their bodies. Cooper, being the observant type, spotted a coot close by. A coot is a nervous little black waterfowl with a skinny neck, bluish-colored feet, and beady orange eyes. When a coot gets surprised or feels threatened, it dives under the water, scuba-swims for 30 to 50 feet, and only resurfaces when it feels it is clear of danger. This passive coot was paddling along minding its own business until the five boys in their custom redneck waders were only a few feet away. For good reason, it was startled and dove under the water, swimming away from the intruders toward the deep part of the river.

"Look at that bird," Coop whispered.

"What about it?" Isaac responded as he concentrated on some discovery of his own.

"It keeps diving under the water and then it comes back up a little ways off. Look! There it goes again!" All the while Cooper had been watching it like a sly cat preparing to pounce. He never took his eyes off the bird. The wheels inside his head were ever turning, calculating time, speed, and accuracy. (The usual type of things a six-year-old boy concerns himself with.) The plans were being laid to catch one more little critter to take home and tame. All at once, out of nowhere, Coop dove down, completely submerging himself in the frigid water.

"What's he doin'? Is he ok?" Levi shouted.

"He's crazy!" another offered.

To all of the boys' astonishment, Coop scrambled to the surface and rose out of the water clutching a skinny coot neck with one hand and clumsily swimming to the bank with the other.

"Holy cow, did you see that?" Spud exclaimed, "He caught that goofy bird!"

"That was cool!" Shawn chimed in.

Once Coop had gotten to his feet and was standing in shallow water, the boys all gathered round to take a look at the confused bird and to congratulate Coop on his fine catch.

"What do you aim to do with it?" Isaac asked.

Being good country kids, they all suggested that he should just let it go. Levi and Isaac were sure enough wowed that he actually caught the coot, but they were not at all surprised that he had tried . . . after all, it was Cooper.

"I'm gonna keep it. I wanna take it home and put it in a cage so I can show everyone," the proud hunter pronounced.

"It's crazy that you caught it Coop and we like seein' it, but that bird don't want to live in a cage. I think you should let it go," Spud said.

"No, I wanna keep it." In true Cooper fashion, he stubbornly refused. By this time his words were choppy as he spoke through chattering teeth. He was soaked to the bone as he stood there wetter than a duck's butt and starting to shiver.

They examined the bird and talked about it for some time. Then out of concern for the coot and to encourage Cooper to hurry on home to get dry before he froze, Spud spoke up. "Come on Coop, you gotta let it go. I tell you what, I'll give you five bucks if you let it go." That got Coop's attention. Now he was thinking, I could catch another coot someday. So for five bucks he consented to turn it loose. Grudgingly, he loosened his grip on the coot and allowed it to struggle away.

Now that the coot was free, their attention turned to the potentially bigger problem. Cooper was getting terribly cold after his swim in the liquid snow. Being the wise older brother and seeing Cooper's predicament, Levi took him by the hand and hurried him toward home saying, "Come on Coop, we've gotta go."

"L-L-L-Levi carry me I-I-I-I'm cold," Coop pleaded as he stumbled to his little knees.

"You gotta keep moving," Levi encouraged.

By this time, they were only about a quarter mile from home. Levi helped Coop to his feet and hustled him along. Coop stumbled to his knees several more times until they were half way to home before he completely collapsed. "L-Levi please carry me I h-h-hurts," he begged. As best he could, Levi carried him the rest of the way.

When they finally got to the back door of the house, Cooper was sobbing and shaking uncontrollably. His little teeth were chattering and his lips were turning as blue as that danged coot's feet. Levi finally found himself pounding on the back door and hollering, "Mom! Mom help! Cooper is cold, hurry!"

"What happened?" Momma K asked as she struggled to remove Coop's wet clothes. Levi was attempting to rehearse the whole coot catching episode to Momma K as she filled the tub with warm water.

"He caught a what? But why is he so wet?" In the flurry to help Cooper, the story was not making much sense to her.

Once in the warm water, Coop complained, "It stings. Ouch! It h-h-hurts. It's too hot."

Momma K knew better—it was only warm water but to a freezing little feller it felt scorching.

"Now what did you catch again? How did you catch it?" quizzed Momma K.

"I c-c-caught a c-c-c-coot, it was r-real fast b-b-but I c-caught it."

She talked with him to try and distract him from being cold and to help him settle down. Gradually, he was shaking less and less and his color was coming back as he slowly thawed out. Finally back to his old self, he announced, "Spud is paying me five bucks though, I think it was worth that. Don't you, Mom?"

Later, when Pops returned home, Levi filled him in. "Dad, I knew if he didn't hurry and walk and keep moving, he would keep gettin' colder, so I made him walk real fast. He made it about halfway home before he gave out, so then I had to carry him the rest of the way. Did I do good, Pops?"

Pops was understandably proud. "You did just right, Levi. Thanks for lookin' after your brother. Keep up the good work." There's something good about seeing things just as they are, Chief Brown Horse, you keep it up, Pops thought.

Cooper learned a healthy respect for frigid water that day and he never went diving for coots in April again. Yet Pops and Momma K knew more of those same kinds of experiences with Cooper were ever waiting just around the bend. In fact, catching the coot was barely the beginning. From then on, Cooper became more skilled

"Fowl Play"

at catching waterfowl, including wild baby ducks and geese, and he did it all barehanded, too. Every so often, he could be seen coming up the pasture with a wild duck held tightly under his arm. He'd reach Pops or Momma K and ask, "Can I keep it?" Occasionally they relented. He'd tame the critters as best as he could, then ultimately set them free. His thrill wasn't in keeping them but in catching them. It was sort of like his own "Catch and Release" program.

It was because of these situations that Pops found himself repeating what he himself had heard many times as a young boy from Grandpa Eddy. "If I take one boy along with me to help, we can get a full day's work done. If I take two boys along, I get about half a day's work done. If I have three boys show up, we get nothin' done at all." That was so true. Stories were lived and all kinds of memories were made because Pops had three boys and one little girl always in tow.

A couple of years later and on another fowl occasion, Cooper and Shawn were playing in another nearby river and they came across some long-necked, funny-walking ducks. As they stalked them, Shawn whispered, "Do you think we can catch'em?"

Coop popped off, "Looks like sittin' ducks to me. They'll be lots easier to catch than coots are. Let's go get a gunny sack first, to carry 'em in."

Upon returning to the stream, they stealthily snuck around with the bag, catching those funny ducks until they had captured every one of them. Soon after, they came marching up the pasture toward the house. They were hauling a squirming grain sack filled with eight ducks in all. "Look what we got! Ain't they funny lookin' things?" Coop said as they pulled the ducks out of the sack one by one. He was all puffed up for having once again bagged "wild ducks."

Those ducks looked unusual all right, not like any wild ducks Pops had ever seen. They were tall and skinny and they stood straight up. When they waddled around in a group, they looked like a bunch of toppling bowling pins. "Cooper, I don't think those ducks are native to this area," Pops offered.

They weren't all bent over like other ducks they were used to seeing, these ducks looked like they were designed for running, not flying or sitting on the water. They looked almost like comical Dr. Seuss characters. With the help of Momma K, they looked them up in a bird book and learned that the ducks were called Indian Runners and were indeed not native to the area.

Coop and Shawn innocently started bragging around town about the great catch they had made. They figured that they were real safari-type hunters now because they had discovered and bagged some exotic critters that nobody in the area had ever seen before. But if they weren't native to the area, just where did they come from?

It wasn't long before Miss Judy showed up at the house in her big red Cadillac. Miss Judy was nice enough alright, but it was common knowledge that you don't want to cross her. It was believed that if she got heated up, she could make a Grizzly Bear turn tail and run. Once in the yard, she got out of her car and said to the first kid she saw, "I want to see Cooper. Is he around here?"

Just then he happened to come around the corner of the house. Bad timing on his part. She turned to face him, and arms crossed said in her stern way, "Cooper, I heard that you caught some odd-looking ducks?" She tilted her head, her direct eyes were accusing.

He listened nervously then mustered up the courage to say, "Oh really?"

Pops always thought there was something healthy about letting a stranded kitten hang on the end of a swaying tree branch a while before it's rescued. The experience just may help it learn a valuable lesson about getting itself stranded. Well, this little kitten was sure enough stranded and hopefully getting an education. Coop didn't know if he should run, tell a story, or just take the imminent whipping. He did none of the above. He just stood there frozen in his tracks, wondering what would come next.

Obviously the duck bagger's news had made its way upstream to the Rockin' H. That was Miss Judy's place, where she kept all sorts of fancy pet ducks and coincidently some had recently gone missing. It was looking like Cooper and Shawn's big haul may have been some of her favorite ducks.

After Coop had appropriately squirmed for a time, Miss Judy

raised her brows and with a slight twinkle in her eye, she continued, "A while back those little waddlers decided to go on a downstream adventure and they never came back. Well, I've been wanting to catch those ducks for months now and put them back in my pond, but I haven't been able to even get close to them. I put them in there to keep the moss and the bugs in check."

Still not quite sure where he stood with her, Coop just replied with an intelligent, "Oh?"

With her hands still on her hips she started in again, "Now, I know you caught those ducks and you thought they were wild so obviously you think they're yours. But I know exactly where they came from and I really want them back."

The tension was lessening a little, so Coop offered an uncertain, "Uh huh."

Miss Judy continued, "So here's what we're gonna do. I'll pay you good if you'll hand them over to me so I can put them back in my pond where they belong."

Coop was still a little stunned, yet relieved and quite happy to hand them over. He came back with a simple, "Sure, that sounds good to me."

She added, "I think there are a few more and if you can catch them, I'll pay you for those, too."

Cooper quickly enlisted the help of his friends and brothers. (He got all his ducks in a row, you could say.) And soon they had caught the rest of Judy's ducks. They delivered sacks of ducks to The

Rockin' H to collect their bounty. The boys turned the ducks loose in Judy's pond where they could live happily ever after gorging on bugs and moss.

Pops said to Momma K, "How does that happen? Cooper wrangles someone else's ducks, gets caught red-handed, then without reservation they pay him a bounty to get them back? I don't get it."

There was a trend in Cooper's life of making connections with critters and people and then having it all turn out well in the end. Over time Cooper had puppies, rabbits, chicks, pigeons, and more. His heart was like a big house and in it he cherished and shepherded all the forlorn critters that he could find, each one having its own little room. But the biggest room in his growing heart was spoken for. He was saving it for the pony he longed to have someday.

"Barnyard Parade"

When backyards were barnyards,
Hay barns were turned into kis' huts.
Fenced fields for baseball, ditches for swimming,
And driveways were two muddy ruts.

The Fourth of July was picnics and fireworks,
Rodeos, games and small country fairs.
Where friends and relatives coming from town
Would escape from their everyday cares.

Parades had bicycles, horses and wagons,
And floats with people well-known.
But out on the farm on the road by the barn,
We'd have a parade of our own.

"Paint Horse"

3. THE PAINTED PONY

The summer before Cooper started grade school, Dr. John stopped by the house. He was a good friend of the family and over the years Pops had trained several horses for him. Dr. John got out of his truck.

"Hey, I have a pony with me that needs some ridin'. He just needs to be tuned up. I would like this little grey ready for my future grandkids to ride," Dr. John explained to Pops. He called the pony grey but it was more plain white than anything. Sort of like a blank painter's canvas, you could say.

"He looks too little for me to ride," Pops joked. "He sure can use some trimmin' down. He's pretty fat. I'm sure my boys would like to ride him for you," Pops offered.

Dr. John was a really good guy. Chances are that the real story was that his kids had outgrown the pony and it was just not being used. Being the nice man that he was, he probably felt like Cooper and his brothers should be able to ride a pony for a while, one just their size. The pony was unloaded and Dr. John drove away.

"What's the pony's name?" Coop asked.

"I don't know if he has a name. I guess you can call him whatever you want," Pops replied.

"I want to call him Banjo. I think it sounds good and you know what else, Pops? He's just about my size," Coop beamed.

"Well he did come to get retuned so the name Banjo fits him pretty good," Pops agreed.

Banjo and Cooper became quick friends. This pony was much easier for him to climb up on than his current horse, Lily, and it wasn't near as far down when it came time to bail off. However, the most important thing for Cooper was that this new pony could run like the wind and jump logs like a bounding jackrabbit. In no time, and with just a little help from his brothers, Coop had Banjo going very well and he was also slimming down. Plus Lily was getting a well-deserved rest.

Besides training horses, Pops painted and sold cowboy pictures to make ends meet. Since he worked at home, he was usually around for all kinds of adventures and he always had a camera close by. He was ever ready to capture references and ideas for future paintings. This was one day that he was glad he was prepared.

"Annie, you know that picture that's hanging in Pops' art room?" Coop asked.

"Which one? There's a whole bunch," she responded.

"The one on the Paint Horse book. It's the one with the guy painting the paint horse markings on the mostly uncolored horse?" Cooper explained.

"Do you mean the one on the horse magazine?" she asked.

"Yeah that's the one I was thinkin' of," Coop said as he continued on. "Do you think people really do that?"

"I remember seein' horses on the TV shows that Indians had painted," Annie offered.

"Maybe people do that, but it seems kind of like a silly thing. It might be fun to try though!" Coop teased.

"We'd have to make it look real good," Annie concluded with her ever-innocent sense of fashion and design. Cooper and Annie were toying with a bright, colorful idea.

The magazine was in fact called the American Paint Horse Journal, and the cover showed a man painting some paint horse markings onto an otherwise colorless horse. It was a humorous image simply making a play on the name "Paint Horse."

So Cooper and his ever-willing accomplice and partner in fun decided to make the idea their own. In Banjo, they had an otherwise colorless horse that they could surely improve upon. He was their blank painter's canvas.

They searched through the shed and found some old red barn paint and a couple of used brushes. Then they set out to make their own "painted pony." Sort of like the one in the painting, but more like the ones that they had seen the Indians in the movies ride. They were making a real honest-to-goodness warhorse out of Banjo. Due to a patient and partially exhausted pony, Cooper and Annie had no trouble creating with their brushes and bare hands a "truly moving" masterpiece.

When Pops and Momma K heard the words, "Come and see," they were not at all prepared for what their eyes saw before them. It was

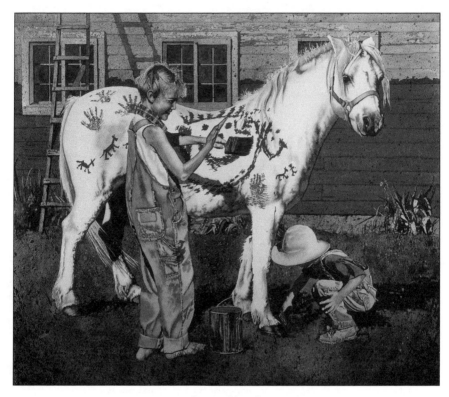

"Painted Pony"

a colorful idea all right. Those kids were laughing and giggling and were into red fun clear up to their elbows. There were handprints, paint splatters, sweeping brush strokes, and smiley faces. And those were just the marks that ended up on the little pony's blank canvas body.

"What are you doin'?" Pops asked, as if he didn't know.

"We are just artisting," Annie said in her innocent, lovable way.

"Do you like it?" they chimed in unison.

"I sure do," Pops replied with an amused grin, but how could he not?

As crazy as it was, nobody in their right mind could get upset at the playful, creative scene. Besides, Pops had unknowingly given them the idea. He just shook his head, grabbed his camera, and set out to capture the scene. Their brother, Levi, "Chief Brown Horse," surely wouldn't approve of this.

I have a pretty painted pony
He has paint from tail to head
I got my pretty painted pony
From paint intended for the shed

Afterwards, the kids gave washing the red paint out of the pony's white hair a real "cowboy" try. Soap and water did take care of most of the youthful artwork, but ultimately the cleanup proved to be a job for time, several rainstorms, and many long sessions of Banjo rolling in the pasture grass. His light red body stood out in the pasture and was silhouetted against the backdrop of an azure sky. With a slight stretch of the imagination, he could be thought of as looking rather patriotic. But to tell the truth, mostly he just looked pink.

During the next month or so, many cars would slow down on the road near the pasture or go speeding past then stop, turn around, and come back to take another look at the rather unusual sight. Pops had a horse breeding friend named Larry who liked to

"A Horse of a Different Color"

raise and sell many different colors of horses. He had black ones and crazy-marked painted ones and he also had all kinds of roans, strawberry, red, bay, and blue. They were all beautiful. Larry always said, "If I could figure out a way to breed a pink horse it would be a show stopper and I would be a millionaire." After this experience, Pops knew Larry was right because that pink pony was a thing that people sure liked to look at.

On one particularly warm afternoon under that same azure sky and in the same pasture, the shifting breeze was light and cotton candy clouds stretched and drifted across the horizon. It was one of those days you just feel lucky to be alive.

Pops was riding ol' Slick, a smart-moving, jet-black, four-stocking-legged Quarter Horse with a wide symmetrical blaze running down the center of his face between a pair of alert, yet kind eyes. Pops was checking the fence around the small, half-grazed pasture near the old house when a slight ruckus disturbed the moment's serenity. The excitement never ends, Pops thought.

Momma K called out, "Cooper, where are you going?" as he bolted past the kitchen window, across the backyard, and down the pasture toward the tack shed. "We'll be eatin' soon, so don't be late for dinner!" she called again.

Without losing his stride, Cooper hollered back, "I'm just goin' to ride Banjo for a minute! I'll be back in time for supper, I promise!"

It's hard for a boy that age and inclination to think of supper when a more enticing feast of tasty adventure has been laid out before him. Pops smiled as he watched Coop scamper through the field, a quiver full of arrows on his back and a willow bow in his hand. The wooden sword strapped to his side flapped back and forth hard enough to nearly trip him. By his side was the family's faithful cow dog, Belle. She was a blue merle Australian Shepherd with copper and white trim and a discerning gleam in her pretty brown eyes. To be truthful, she had one pretty brown eye and one half foggy, sort of milky-white and blind.

It had been scarred by a stray BB from one wild young cowboy's Red Rider. However, she was a forgiving and constant protector.

Pops said out loud to himself, "Does he know how lucky he is or does he think all boys can just saddle up and ride off over a thousand acres of river bottoms to chase bad guys and rescue fair maidens while searching for lost treasures?"

Pops galloped alongside the little runaway, his well-worn oxbow stirrups creaking and the saddle leather complaining as he shifted his weight to one side. Slick braced himself as Pops reached down and put his hand under Coop's arm and hoisted the little feller up on the saddle in front of him.

Pops asked, "Where you off to in such a hurry, little man?"

Cooper gasped, "This is way high up here, as high as Lily!" Then he answered the question. "I just got stuff to do. Can you help me saddle Banjo?"

"How do you like bein' way up here on ol' Slick?" Pops asked.

"It makes me feel way tall."

Isaac on Slick

"That's a good feelin' huh? You remember how this feels. If you always try to ride tall in the saddle, throughout your life things will mostly be good for you." Pops encouraged as he referred to the little boy's future. Even though Coop didn't fully understand what Pops meant by the statement, he shook his head in agreement.

Undaunted, he again pressed, "Still, can you help me?"

Pops answered, "Sure I can, let's go saddle that pony so you can practice sittin' up tall." Cooper was soon mounted and riding off into his future.

When autumn rolled around it was time to take Banjo back home. He was mostly white again, so luckily there wasn't too much explaining to do. It was a good thing that Dr. John was a real nice, understanding guy though.

After Banjo left and went back home, Cooper's pony-sickness got worse. He continued to be consumed with the idea of having one of his own. He had gotten a taste of what he wanted and he liked it. Even though Pops hadn't given in yet, he was beginning to soften. He had to admit there were benefits when it came to having

a pony. It was easier for Cooper to saddle up all on his own. He could climb on without help and of course there was that recurring thought that there was less distance to fall.

Over the next year or two, more ponies came to be trained to ride and pull carts. Sugar Plum, Ninya, Roany,

Stumpy, Buttercup, Daisy, and Bow were some of the favorites. On one occasion, there was even a spotted burro named Pedro that Levi, Isaac, and Cooper rode, but sadly, in Coop's words, none of the ponies got to stay for keeps. Having this array of potbelly critters enter and exit their lives just added to Coop's longing to have one. One that he could call his very own.

"American Paint Horse"
(How's your geography?)

"Feed My Sheep"

4. ANGEL PRECIOUS

"Here she comes!" Cooper squealed.

"Here who comes?" the whole family asked, almost in unison, sounding like an out-of-tune choir.

"Oh, it must be Sally," Momma K offered. Sally was Cooper's new friend, but he seemed to have a new friend almost every day. Sally lived just across the valley. She was a kind, even-tempered, and highly educated older lady. She lived alone except for three noisy dogs, a mixed flock of Churro sheep, and several head of horses. Her animals were her family and she nearly wore herself out caring for them. She and Cooper were similar when it came to accumulating forlorn animals.

The sheep herd that Sally owned was, for the most part, unchecked. Her horses and sheep lived in the same pasture year round. As a result, the horses all had the same hairdo—their ponytails were all cropped to the same length, head high to a sheep. When it was cold and the snow got deep, the sheep, out of hunger and boredom, would chew on the horses' tails. While it didn't really hurt the horses, it did make them look odd, all of them sporting the same "Dutch boy" back-door haircut.

For a driveway, Cooper's family shared a bumpy dirt lane with the hay farmer next door. Sally would often come bouncing down the lane in her mint green 1963 Ford pickup. She would come to get a load of hay to feed her critters. The cab would be full of frantic dogs jumping from the floor to the seat. Then they'd climb over Sally to poke their heads out the driver's side window, barking all the while.

When Coop would hear Sally coming down the driveway, he'd run to the door to see while shrugging off his mother's attempts to stop him. When Sally spotted him, she would wave her hands enthusiastically as she pulled into the farmyard and backed up to the haystack.

Cooper followed Sally around, jabbering, "What are your dogs' names? How many sheep do you have? Do you ride your horses? Why not? How much hay do you need? Did you know that your truck is the same color as the hay?" He offered a barrage of questions that could not really be answered. Sally was patient and answered as best she could.

"Where have you been? Whatchya' been doin'?" On and on he'd go. Being too small himself to lift a bale of hay, he would just make himself comfortable sitting on the hay stack. While he talked and watched her load the truck, it was obvious that he had looked forward to another visit with her and that she liked seeing him, too. In the course of things, Sally told Coop all about her animals, especially one favorite lamb named Angel Precious.

As their friendship grew, Cooper said, "I want to invite Sally to my birthday party. Do you think she'll come?"

"Do you mean our birthday party?" Pops shot back.

"Oh yeah. That's what I meant. Still, do you think she would come?"

"It wouldn't hurt to ask and see what happens," Pops encouraged.

Sadly, she was unable to attend, but later she brought Cooper a nice gift. She knew how to make the boy feel important and he could hardly wait for her to come again.

On one visit, Sally told Coop that she wanted to give him a lamb to call his very own. At first, Pops and Momma K thought it was fine as long as Sally kept the lamb at her farm and Cooper could just call it his. He visited the lamb at Sally's place several times, usually alongside his brothers. Over the course of the summer months, Sally began subtly suggesting that Cooper take the lamb home. Pops imagined a storybook image of a darling little bleating, curly-wooly lamb. After much pleading from Coop, Pops finally consented to go see the lamb, not realizing that it had been quite some time since it was first offered.

"Three of a Kind"

As a general rule, cattle ranchers and sheep farmers don't see eye to eye. It's not necessarily good or bad, it just tends to be two different schools of thinking and Pops thought of himself as part of the cattle ranchers' camp.

The best experience they ever had with sheep was when the family was in Copper Mountain, Colorado, at an art show and music festival called "West Fest." In conjunction with the three-day event, there was a kid rodeo. Pops was setting up the art show while the kids were off playing.

"Dad, Dad! There's a rodeo here!" said Levi and Isaac as they tugged at him. "Can we ride in it? Dad, we know how. Let us ride, it will be fun, come on, please."

Little Cheyenne was right behind them with the same plea, "Daddy, Daddy, can I ride one, too?"

How could he say no to that?

Cooper was too small to participate, but Levi, Isaac, and Annie entered the "Mutton Bustin'" and some other contests. The boys each won their event. (Yes, Pops was proud.) They were each awarded a brand new pair of Justin cowboy boots, so they were justifiably hooked on riding sheep.

Cheyenne, on the other hand, won the show. She was so little that she could not grip the critter's wool and hang on the same way as the boys. She was such a trooper and always wanted to be there with her guys, even if the task at hand was difficult. "Daddy help me!" she said.

Pops got in the chute with her and positioned her on the sheep.

Facing backwards, she lay down on its back, turned her head sideways, and squished her little cheek into the nose-tickling wool. She then wrapped her legs around the critter's neck, crossed her feet in a firm grasp, and sunk her little hands deep into the critter's soft flanks. She was there to stay. When the gate was opened, she stuck to that sheep like stink sticks to a skunk. The crowd hooped and hollered as she circled the arena on a runaway sheep. The only way she came off was for Pops to chase her down and tell her it was okay to let go. She won the hearts of the entire crowd. Pops lifted her high in the air and as she waved to the fans, they all cheered back.

So sheep are good for something—just keep them in a little kids' rodeo or in someone else's pastures and the cattlemen and the sheep farmers will all get along.

After Pops finally agreed to visit Cooper's lamb, the little boy was relentless in asking when they could go. "Dad, let's go to Sally's and see Angel Precious. Come on, you promised!" he insisted.

"Did I say I would go see your sheep?" Pops teased.

"Yes, you did! You know you did, and I want to bring him home so I can have him here."

"Him?" Pops had assumed Angel Precious was a girl name.

"No, he's a him and you knew it," Coop retorted.

"Well I guess I never really gave it much thought," Pops said as he shrugged it off.

Pops and Coop finally picked a day and went over to Sally's place to see the little lamb. They ended up being there for quite a long time. When they finally returned, Cooper's mother asked with taunting in her voice, "So are we gonna be sheep farmers now?"

All Pops could do was reply with stubborn conviction, "No. Did you know anything about that sheep?" he asked, eyeing her with suspicion.

Momma K said, "Well, it's just a little lamb. Isn't it? I don't see what it could hurt to let Cooper bring it home. You know 'Mary had a little lamb,' surely Cooper could, too. What would it hurt? Besides, it was such a nice gesture on Sally's part to offer it to him and we surely don't want to offend her, do we?" She said it all in a hurry and in a way that Pops was not supposed to refute.

Sternly, he attempted to set her straight. "Cooper's lamb is a full-grown musky, Churro ram with four fully curled horns and long, dirty wool. A name like 'Angel Precious' does not accurately describe the animal that Sally offered. No, we are not going to be sheep farmers. I like cuddly little lambs as much as anyone, but there was nothing cute or cuddly about the sheep I just saw!"

"Oh," Momma K said with thoughtful surprise. "I didn't even think that it has been a while since Sally gave him the lamb. I guess it has grown up in the meantime."

"That is true," Pops replied. In this instance he expected everyone to understand that no meant absolutely not! And that was the end of it. "It's not that sheep are all bad, but they don't fit into our program, so if we brought it here it would just be trouble. It's like an old feller once said, 'All the horses at the horse sale aren't bad horses, but all bad horses do go through the horse sale.'" Pops wanted to stick to the familiar, and for him that was horses.

When it was all said and done, they all got a good laugh out of it. But it was starting to look like giving in and allowing Cooper to have a pony wasn't such a bad idea after all. Maybe then he wouldn't be tempted to bring all sorts of other critters home.

Could a young boy be clever enough to consciously set a chain of events into motion so that he could actually get what he'd always wanted?

"Shade of Grey"

5. THE RANGE CAMP

With all notions of ever being sheep farmers being done away with, it was time to get back to riding horses and working cows. Like cowboys are supposed to do.

The kids asked endless questions about Pops' childhood. "Tell us about when you and Grandpa Eddy stayed in his old range camp when you were little," they'd say.

Pops reminisced, "Yeah, those were good times."

"Oh come on, tell us more," they'd prod.

"I think I've already told you all the stories. I don't think there's any more to tell."

"Just tell us about when you and Grandpa Eddy would go campin' in his range camp."

"Well . . . okay. You know the times weren't always perfect, campin' in that thing. I remember tryin' to sleep, my legs curled up in a ball and my back aching. You see the bed wasn't very big and I'd be crowding the window at the back of the camp. I'd also be tryin' to get fresh air but the window only opened a sliver. It was stuck, it hadn't been fully opened in years. And the wooden track that it was supposed to slide in had layers of old dried paint caked in it, and that kept it from sliding."

"Why did you need fresh air so much?" Annie asked with concern in her voice.

"Because it would get pretty cold at night. During the deer hunts. I'd have about twenty pounds of quilts piled on top of me. All that bedding only added to the cramped feeling and I felt like I needed some fresh air so I could breathe better."

"But I thought you could build a fire," Levi said.

"That's just it, during a restless night's sleep, I'd look over my shoulder and I'd see Grandpa Eddy's silhouette framed in the glowin' firelight from the little old cook stove. From beneath the weight of the old quilts I'd watch him as he stoked the fire in preparation to brew hot chocolate, bake biscuits, and fry some eggs. The cook stove's loose joints and sloppy fittin' dampers leaked just enough firelight to illuminate his weathered face and squinted eyes."

"That sounds warm and cozy," Annie said.

"Oh it was. In fact, once the fire got goin' it gave off enough heat to warm seven camps, I'm sure. Then the damp canvas cover stretched over the antique wooden bows of the camp roof would give off the odors of years on the range both good and bad. But that smell was

mostly outweighed by the sweat-soaked saddle blankets that were stuffed under the cook stove. They were there to dry out and to torture me, so it seemed."

"Those were good times?" Isaac asked.

"Well they got better as soon as the cocoa was hot, the eggs were ready, and we put those saddle blankets outside," Pops chuckled.

"We want to do that some time," they all said.

"Eddy's camp is gone and there aren't very many around anymore. But if we're lucky, we'll get a chance to camp in one someday," Pops assured them.

A few days after the range camp quiz, Momma K asked Pops, "Do you know someone named Bill from Kemmerer, Wyoming?"

"I don't think so. Why?" said Pops.

"Well, he called and he left his number so I said you would call him. All he said was his name and he was calling from Kemmerer. From the sound of it, it seemed like he knew you."

"Wonder what he wants?" Pops was curious.

"He said something about herding some cows in Wyoming. Give him a call."

"Alright," Pops said as he picked up the phone and dialed.

"This is Bill Kennedy."

"Hi, I'm returnin' your call from earlier today," Pops said.

Bill explained, "A neighbor of mine is a friend of yours and he said you and your boys may be interested in doin' some cattle work?" He went on to say, "I am runnin' a bunch of cows and calves on some leased ground here in Kemmerer and my herder has up and quit on me. So I'm lookin' for some help for the rest of the season or at least until I can find a fulltime replacement."

Pops thought, Shoots yah! We're always lookin' for more cow work.

"What did Bill want?" Momma K asked.

"He's lookin' for someone to come and ride herd on his cattle for awhile."

"Why don't you go and take the boys? It could be a great experience for them," she encouraged.

Levi and Isaac were close enough to hear and they were always happy to work cows. "Can we go, Pops? Let's go!"

Pops told Bill that they would be there as soon as they could.

Bill said, "Don't worry about bringin' any horses, we have several that my herder was usin'. They should do fine for you."

It was clear that Bill was saying, "Don't take time with roundin' up horses. Just put yourselves together and come help me, and anytime won't be too soon." Early the next morning they loaded up their gear, jumped old Belle in the truck, and headed over the mountains to Wyoming. They left early so Annie and Cooper wouldn't feel bad about being left behind. When they awoke, Momma K relieved their disappointment by promising that next time they could go, too.

After a two-hour drive, Bill met them at the range near Kemmerer where his cattle were located and said, "Just follow me." They made their way through the hills another hour or so from the highway to the cow camp. The camp was great. It was an old range camp or sheep wagon just like Pop's description of Grandpa Eddy's. And there was a two-wheeled commissary hooked on behind it for hauling extra supplies.

The camp was stocked with firewood and food and there were four horses waiting for them. They had brought their own saddles and gear. Bill showed them around the range and filled them in on where they needed to keep the cows moving and the areas that he did not want the cattle to wander into. After they had their instructions, Bill waved goodbye.

They looked at each other and said, "Now what?"

The boys said, "It's still daylight, let's saddle up and explore this place." They rode for a couple of hours and made a pretty good circle to get their bearings. Once back at the camp, they built a fire in the stove and cooked supper, stew and apple pie. They ate until they were stuffed. Then they fed Belle the dinner leftovers in a dish under the camp. She curled up on a pile of saddle blankets, blankets that were not going underneath the cook stove. She bedded down for the night.

Pops cracked the back window open a little, this window worked! They laid out bedrolls and snuggled in for the night. Pops said, "We're cowboyin' for real boys. Now lets' see if we can get some sleep."

The next morning, they awoke to the chilly mountain air along with a skiff of frost on the ground. Pops sent the boys out to feed the horses while he built another fire in the stove, then he scrambled some eggs in an old cast iron frying pan. He toasted bread right on the bare top of the cook stove, just like he had remembered doing with Grandpa Eddy.

The camp was facing east so as the sun rose over the mountaintops, the bright orange light flooded in the open door, warming the air and the camp. It felt so good. With the warming of the sun, the frost disappeared. When the horses were done eating, it was time to saddle  up and ride. They filled their canteens and tied them to their saddle horns then packed a lunch in their saddlebags. This was livin'!

The boys then asked, "Which way are we goin'?"

"Let's take a look," Pops said as they made a plan according to a map that Bill had left. "I think we should head south and make a big circle to the East around this ridge, then go just beyond the ponds," Pops said as he drew with his finger the plan he was describing. "Then across the flats you see here and up this draw. I think that will take us most of the day and it should bring us right back to the camp."

"Sounds good," Levi agreed. "Let's go!"

They rode all morning in the direction they had planned, straight away from the camp. There were some sensitive areas on this range that Bill wanted the cattle to stay out of. As is typical with cattle, and some people, they constantly want to drift toward those forbidden areas. It was the cowboy's job to push and keep the cattle back. It's sort of like a kid (or a husband) in a grocery store. They always drift toward the candy aisle and regularly need to be intercepted and herded back to the healthy food. Along the way, the boys found and easily moved a few bands of cattle back to where they belonged.

At midday, they started to bend their path in a large circle back toward the camp. It was time to pick a spot in the grass to get down and have some lunch. As Pops sat there on a small flat rock he leaned back against a spruce tree, eating a sandwich and watching the kids gobble down their food. The air was still and quiet and he thought to himself, does it get any better than this? Not in my book.

As they mounted up to complete the afternoon loop, Pops said, "We can cover a little more ground if we split up." They all agreed that it was a good idea, so off they went. Pops had to keep reminding himself that even though these boys were mighty ambitious, they were still just nine and ten years old. They were just little fellers, so he didn't want to let them get too far out of his sight.

Late in the afternoon, they came to one of those sensitive areas and as expected, there were about twenty pairs of cattle grazing there. As they attempted to push them, the cattle would circle back behind the boys. So they had to really get after the cattle hard to herd them down the country. Levi was quite a distance ahead of Pops and Isaac and he had a cantankerous cow on the run. They were going fast and were headed straight for a washed out ditch. The cow horse that Levi was riding was willing and doing everything he could to keep that cow moving in the right direction. As they were just about to go over a small rise and possibly, drop out of Pops' line of sight, they encountered the ditch. Instinctively, the horse, amid full stride, lunged forward with all his force and jumped the wide ditch, clearing it easily. All the while Levi was focused on the cow. He was leaning way up in the saddle and watching close. He was not prepared for what came next. Riding in a saddle that was too big for him, he was bouncing and slopping around. Along with being caught off guard, he was launched in a different direction than the horse was jumping in. In short, they parted company.

Levi went tumbling. Pops couldn't see what happened but when he finally saw the riderless horse he was worried and hoped Levi wasn't hurt. Pops left the cows that he and Isaac were pushing and raced to where Levi had landed. As Pops got closer he feared for the worst. Is he hurt? Pops wondered. Levi was still lying face down. His body was quivering and shaking like someone unconscious and very badly hurt.

As Pops got closer he slid off of his horse and knelt by Levi. He wasn't sure what he should do next. Should he move him? "Levi, are you okay, can you hear me?" he asked in what was possibly a panicked voice. When Pops was close enough to better assess the whole situation he, could hear that Levi was making some pitchy noises. "Levi, talk to me," Pops almost ordered, in a panic. Just then Isaac galloped up on his horse.

Being catapulted off of a speeding horse can easily ruin one's whole day, but this was no time to be messin' around. Right then, Levi rolled over with a big grass-stained smile spread across his face. His hat brim was pushed up in the front like the bugler on the old western, comedy show, F-troop. It was only then that Pops realized that the indefinable sounds that he had been making were laughter muffled by a mouth full of grass and weeds. His laughter explained the body shaking. Levi had landed in the middle of a big soft stand of grass and tumbled head over heels, not getting hurt in the least. Levi thought it must have looked so funny, and enjoyed the fact that he could hear Pops speeding toward him frantically hollering and being overly concerned. So Levi chose to just lie there, laughing and waiting.

Pops wasn't sure if he should hug him or beat him. He chose the hug. Isaac caught Levi's horse. As Pops helped him to his feet, Levi brushed himself off then climbed back into that sloppy saddle.

As they rode on and finished the day's work, they reflected on and laughed about the company parting episode. Laughing, Levi announced, "I will have a saddle of my own some day. One built just for me. A custom one and it will fit just right even if I have to build it myself."

As the boys chattered about their cowboy dreams and other aspirations, a kind of pride came over ol' Pops, the kind that causes one to sit straight up in the saddle and take notice of all the good things that surround you.

After four days, the permanent replacement arrived so it was time to pack up and return home. As they drove out to the highway the boys said, "Pops, next time let's bring Mom, Annie, and Cooper! That would be way more fun. But we will need two camps to fit us all."

"We'll have to work on that," Pops told them.

Annie ready for the next outing

6. LILY

Life was lived and a fun easy pace,
In all his boyhood reflection.
Many good times were there to be had,
With a pony to make the connection.

He soared with eagles, scouted the prairie,
Finding where the buffalo roam.
He raced for the gold cup at a fan-filled track,
Or at least fresh baked cookies from home.

Lily was the first horse that Cooper got to claim as his own. An old retired roping mare, she was a chestnut color with a wide white blaze down the middle of her face, two white hind feet, and a Circle K brand on her left shoulder—a cold brand that had grown in with white hair. She was a little stoved-up in her front end from years of calf roping, but she had a willing heart and could still move well enough. In Cooper's eyes she was a beautiful, sleek, stocking-legged sorrel friend that he could ride anywhere, if he could just get up on her back. Over time, as a protector, Lily proved to be worth her weight in gold.

"Dad, Mom, Levi, anybody, can somebody help me?" Cooper often called out. "I need help putting a saddle on Lily, I need to ride her."

This was a regular request as he wanted to explore the hills and meadows hunting for wild cattle, searching for desperadoes, and keeping the range safe for everyone. Cooper was rarely patient enough to wait for someone to come along and help him. A little cowboy often has important places to be and endless urgent jobs to get done.

On a certain occasion no one was available to help him and, as usual, he was anxious to get going. Pops happened to look out the kitchen window on a scene that caught his full attention. All by himself, Coop had rustled up a halter and rope. He then caught Lily in the pasture, and tied her to the fence.

Now, if one knows anything about horses, their natural tendencies, and their self-preservation instincts, the episode that

followed is nothing short of amazing. Had Pops not seen it for himself, he may not have believed it.

Using a crude slipknot, Cooper tied Lily's head to an old cedar fence post that was strung with barbed wire. He tied it low and short so he could climb up two wires and swing onto Lily's head, sitting just behind her ears. Once he was facing forward and "safely" on this precarious perch, he reached out and carefully pulled the loose end of the knot, untying the rope from the post. Lily stood there with her eyes wide and her ears pricked but never moving a muscle. Pops, watching from the window, didn't move a muscle either. He was torn between hurrying to Coop's rescue or staying put. Pops feared what may happen to Coop if this scenario were to spin out of control. At the same time, he feared spooking the horse and being the cause of potential disaster. Luckily, the "rescue reflex" in Pops was restrained, and he remained frozen in place.

Once free to move, Lily cautiously raised her head, lifting Cooper high in the air as he methodically scooted down her neck and over her withers. All the while he was clutching the loose end of the lead rope. He gradually found his way onto her bare back and into position to go about his important business of cowboyin'.

This scene was perfected and repeated many times over the next couple of years. Every time Cooper climbed upon Lily's head and down her neck it was a powerful moment of union between friends. They had an unspoken yet obvious two-way trust. The possible danger of a ranch-type wreck in this situation was very real. On one hand it looks cute and harmless. It's sort of like running your hand along the typically harmless smooth strands of a barb wire fence then instantly things can go all wrong. When you get distracted or slip and are abruptly pierced by the occasional sharp barbs, the pain is real and lasting.

This moment, no doubt was one that had to be handled carefully. Lily tenderly accommodated and watched over Coop the same way she had her own wobbly-legged foals in the past. But, no matter how he got on her back, with a saddle or not, he was there and it was time to ride, the faster the better.

One day early in October, Pops overheard Cooper and Momma K

having what sounded like a serious talk. By the tone of Cooper's voice, it sounded like an important discussion.

"Mom, I need a Zorro costume! Could you make one for me?" he said with the accent of intentional hand gestures.

"For what?" she asked.

He said, "Oh, I just want it for Halloween, I guess. But just the same, Mom, could you get it done real fast?"

Cooper then proceeded to explain exactly how he wanted it to look. First, he had to have a long, black, silky cape with a tie string around his neck. Then he wanted a black, flat-brimmed hat with a stampede string and a slide bead to snug up under his chin to secure the hat when he was going fast.

"And I need a fancy sword to hook in my belt."

"I'll get right on that," Momma K promised.

Every day he checked, "Mom, do you have my cape and stuff done yet?"

"I'm workin' on it, Coop but you know I have lots of other things to do too. You'll have to learn some patience."

"But Mom, I need . . ."

"Cooper Grey," she said, looking down at him, "you heard me." When she added his middle name and looked straight at him he knew it was time to leave well enough alone, so for the moment he stopped asking and shuffled off.

The day the costume was finally finished, Cooper put it on with a long-sleeved turtleneck shirt with a racing horse pattern on it. He pulled on some black sweatpants and tucked them into his well-worn cowboy boots with a pair of huge Texas star spurs. Finally, he strapped on his sword. This outfit, in all of its particulars, did not come off for the next three weeks. It was then that Momma K understood. He did not want the costume only for the upcoming Halloween holiday. He needed it to help him look more official when he was out chasing desperadoes on a regular basis.

The costume was made complete by dressing Lily up too. Pops happened to have a small "fancy" saddle that the kids used on special occasions such as parades and rodeos. It was black leather, trimmed with diamond-shaped "silver" spots and the stirrups were covered with long, pointed Spanish tapaderos. It was a saddle just like the ones on the old-timey, coin-operated metal ponies that sat in front of the drugstore. With a similarly showy bridle and reins, horse and rider were outfitted and ready to be on their way. They looked better than any silver-screen heroes, maybe even better than Roy Rogers or the Lone Ranger! Quick as a flash, Cooper could be duded up and turn into a super hero, and he didn't even need a phone booth to do it.

Cooper and Lily raced through river bottoms and across hillsides, chasing foxes, birds, and a myriad of imaginary critters while Coop's black cape flowed and snapped in the wind behind him. It must be noted that all the time he rode and scouted the pastures and meadows, the neighborhood never once had a problem with bandits, robbers, rustlers, dragons, or wild elephants. Nor did Lily have any concerns with getting too fat.

When Pops and "The Wild Bunch" as the kids referred to themselves, mounted up and headed out, Coop was on Lily, Levi and Isaac would be riding their horses, and Pops was usually riding a young colt in training. Each time they left, you could bet they would be coming back with an exciting story to tell. The Wild Bunch explored amid the dogwood willows and swampy bogs, the thick meadow grasses, cattails, toolies, and all the overgrown secret places of the river bottoms. In Pops' reflections it seems like it was just yesterday, and often he wishes it was.

A favorite game they played was "horseback tag." They would ride into the extremely tall grass of the river bottoms, spread out, and the one who was "it" would count to fifty then holler, "Ready or not you shall be caught!" They'd then sneak around and play a sort of hide and go seek on their horses. It was fun for the kids and good exposure for young horses to all kinds of surprises. Sometimes it would get very competitive and creative. They'd do things like hide in the river under the banks, or force their way into the willow thickets. If they got really good they could even lay their horse down in the tall grass and hide forever, but when "Ready or not you shall be caught" was sounded it was all out "Tag you're it!"

After one such day of playing, the boys came back from having an especially exciting ride. When they arrived home, Annie and Momma K were in the kitchen cleaning up. They had just baked chocolate chip cookies and the house was filled with the sweet smells of baking. Annie stood on a stool at the counter as she helped Momma K. They both turned in surprise as Coop exploded into the house. Cooper and Lily were splattered with half-crusted, smelly river mud. Coop was wide-eyed and beaming as he related the adventure to his mother.

"Mom, you shoulda' seen us!" He exclaimed, jumping up and down with excitement. "We was goin' along, playin' tag, the grass was so high you couldn't even see the horses, it looked just like we were floatin' along on the tops of the grass cuz it was so tall. Then all of a sudden, a huge buck with big antlers

jumped up right between me and Pops and started running."

Wide-eyed and focused on the drama, Annie offered, "Do you mean horns?"

"No, Annie, on a cow they're called horns and on a deer they're called antlers, duh," he continued. "Pops said it must have been layin' there just hidin' and we spooked it. We just turned the horses and took off runnin' with it. It was gigantic, Mom! Pops said the horses had no real chance of keepin' up with the big deer, but it was sure fun tryin'!"

He didn't skip a beat. "Anyway we were runnin' with the deer and I was leanin' way up over the saddle horn to help Lily go faster, just like those bull-doggin' cowboys in the rodeo do, you know, where two of em' are chasin' a steer, one on each side of it. Me and Pops were like the cowboys and the deer was like the steer and I'm sure

I coulda dogged it. Then all of a sudden Lily ran plum into a big mud hole. I didn't even see it comin' because the grass was so big and tall. She sunk clear up to her belly. I'm not kidding!" He took a breath. "Mom, she dead stopped and almost dropped clean out of sight then I went sailin' like a rocket, somersaultin' right between her ears and over her head and the reins got jerked right out of my hands!"

"Are you all right?" Momma K asked with some concern.

"Shoot yah! The grass was so long that it was a soft landing. It didn't even hurt. Well, at least it didn't hurt that bad."

Isaac, who had been listening to the whole story, chimed in with a scoffing laugh, "You didn't land in the grass, Coop. Look at yourself! You landed right in the middle of that mud hole."

Coop retorted, "Well, still, it didn't hurt, but the deer did get away. It was so fun! Pops came to see if I was okay because I flew about halfway 'round the world. It was the best wreck I ever had! Then we went back and helped Lily out of that muddy mess. She didn't even throw a fit. She just waited for us to help her out." Turning he asked, "Can we do it again, Dad?"

Pops was listening quietly, secretly proud, as Cooper spilled his tale. He felt the young cowboy from long ago stirring a bit deep inside. Pops replied with only a moment's hesitation, "How about we go tomorrow and see if we can find that old buck again?"

A huge grin spread across Cooper's mud-smudged face as his focus quickly changed. He asked, "Can we have some of those cookies now?"

On another occasion, Coop was racing through the field while Pops was watching. He could see that Coop was sort of losing control of Lily. He had dropped one rein and the other one was too long. She got going faster and faster, and even though it was just for a minute, it was getting scary. Feeling her chance at freedom, the mare headed for the nearest open gate. Coop was hollering "Whoa!" but it was having no effect. She had her sights on greener pastures on the other side of the gate.

The gateway was a small opening, about four feet wide with eight-foot-tall posts on both sides and a crossbar over the top connecting them. Even though he was pulling on the reins and hollering for her to stop, Coop wasn't having any luck getting Lily to slow down. He decided that while going through that gateway he would reach out bare- handed and grab the upright post in order to stop Lily.

That was logical right?

As the two blew through the open gate he applied his plan and in one blurred motion he was jerked off that mare slicker than grease dancing off a hot griddle. Coop landed with a thud. Pops honestly didn't think the little cowboy even knew what had just happened.

Pops hurried to his side as Coop lay there out of breath and shaken, blinking his eyes. Slowly, with Pops' help, he staggered to his feet, one leg at a time. He was half-dazed, mad, rubbing his hurt pride, and probably craving some cookies.

Luckily, in those wrecks he never seemed to get hurt for keeps. Whenever he fell off (and it happened many times), Lily would stop and return to him. She would then patiently wait for Cooper to pick himself up and figure out a way to get back on board. On some occasions he would find no way to get back on so he would come limping home, leading his loyal friend. He surely loved her, and she surely felt some type of affection for him. They became inseparable. The adventures they shared were many. Momma K was grateful to have Lily tending Cooper. She affectionately referred to Lily as "the baby sitter."

Even though his experiences with Lily were timeless, irreplaceable, and allowed him to ride tall in the saddle, Coop still longed for that special pony, the image he constantly held in his mind. He imagined a pony with a long, flowing, flaxen mane and tail. A pony just his size. But to this point that pony just hadn't seemed to come his way. Truth was that Pops just couldn't see much use for ponies. To his mind, ponies were just short, fat, sawed-off troublemakers, not big enough to really do anything useful. He couldn't understand why anyone in his right mind would want one around. Besides, Coop had Lily. Pops was even heard to say, "What more hay-burner could a cowboy want than good ol' Lily? Coop's still a little short on the ground but with Lily, he's sure' nuff ridin' tall in the saddle."

Maybe in all that time it was Pops who was a little "short" sighted.

"Sun Kissed"

7. A LESSON FOR LIFE

Life lessons come in many ways. Some are subtle, like second nature, an experience that just seems to make sense and quietly becomes a part of you. Others may be drastic, unforgettable events. Either way, real life lessons are those that stick and make you who you are.

Pops, Momma K, and the kids had many important and unforgettable lessons come their way. One nearly tragic Fall day, Isaac found himself in the middle of an unwelcome learning experience. It was a time when Pops had a couple of mustangs at the place for training, a big brown gelding and a small buckskin mare. These critters came with some serious baggage because of the way they had been previously handled. They were both very aggressive and mistrusting. You could say they had learned some life lessons of their own. And their learning was all based on self-preservation.

Pops had been working with them for a couple of weeks and they had made good progress. Regardless, he had warned the kids not to approach them. He did not want to take a chance on any of the kids getting hurt. The little mare was extremely wary of people. Pops had been working with her—saddling and riding her a little—but she had a long way to go before she would be safe for the kids to be around. Everything Pops was doing with her was to help her gain trust, respect, and self-confidence. To that point, if Pops relaxed or was not paying attention, she would realize it and strike out at him with her sharp front hooves. She never connected, but if she had, she could have done real damage.

"Hobbled"

It may not have been the best training approach, but sometimes when Pops thought the kids might come around, he would hobble her front feet, just to avoid one of them getting struck. That was his thinking anyway.

These mustangs were pretty wild. If they were turned out in the pasture, they would have no problem going over the fence and running off, so Pops had to keep them in a stall or a corral most of the time. But as skinny as the little mare was, Pops felt bad for her and wanted to put her out on pasture as much as possible to help her gain weight.

On that particular day, the mare was saddled and turned out on some grass near the tack shed. She may as well wear a saddle while she was eating. That way she could get used to it and gain some weight at the same time. She was also hobbled to keep her from striking someone. Isaac, being about 10 years old at the time, was always curious. When he got home from school he finished his lessons and, as usual, he quickly changed his clothes and headed out to ride a horse. Pops noticed him running down the pasture and through the far gate into the area where the little mare was feeding. He started to pass by her. Then, for some reason, he decided to approach her.

"Mustangs"

Pops watched from a distance, hoping things would go well. Isaac was cautiously moving toward the mare with an outstretched hand, offering to pet her. He meant well, but to the little mare his cautious movements must have felt more like a stalking predator than a hopeful friend. She was not very big, but neither was Isaac. With his cowboy hat on his head, he was about the same height as her back. As he got closer to her, she started to shift her weight to her haunches until she looked like a tense coiling snake about to strike its prey. He was almost close enough to touch her nose.

Pops was too far away to stop Isaac or the mare. He tensely waited and hoped for the best. Pops crossed his fingers and thought to himself, the hobbles should keep her from doing anything too crazy, shouldn't they? But unconsciously he found that he had started anxiously walking toward them.

Right then he saw something he'd never seen before and hoped to never see again. It was as if the little mare was consciously recoiling, just enough to draw him in close. Isaac continued to move closer and closer. When he reached out to touch her nose, he found himself within her striking range. In a flash, she reared up wide-eyed, with nostrils flared! She made an eerie squealing sound as she raised the hobbles high in the air and reached out over Isaac's hat. She hooked the hobbles right behind his little neck and jerked back toward herself. It was as quick and smooth and calculated as a pouncing cat on an unsuspecting mouse.

Pops was terrified and raced toward the scene as fast as he could. The pasture grass was tall enough that some of the scene was blocked from his view, but he could see enough to be mighty worried. He feared that the jerk from the hobbles had thrown Isaac face down beneath the little mare. He may be pinned to the ground by the hobbles chain being on his neck. He would be in a helpless position where she could easily stomp him. Now Pops was on a dead run with many things racing through his mind, unsure what he was going to find when he got there. Soon, he was close enough to take in the entire scene.

Thankfully, Isaac was not where Pops feared to find him. As he urgently looked farther, Pops was quite relieved to find that, miraculously, the thrust of the hobbles did not pin Isaac down to the ground. Instead, the motion was so forceful that it sent him tumbling head-over-heels right between the mare's hind legs and beyond. Then he had continued to roll until he bounced right up on his feet. He was all mixed up, not sure where he was or what had just happened. He was behind the little mare and facing away from her, but she was not done. One could say she came up empty handed, so she sat back on her haunches again, this time whirling around to find Isaac. She was now reaching out again with her front feet and was attempting another strike.

Pops instinctively yelled for Isaac to run. Isaac, while slightly looking over his shoulder, was able to respond just in time to flee beyond her second attempt to clothesline him. At nearly that same moment, Pops jumped the fence and got to Isaac. He scooped him up and moved him a safe distance from the mare. Once they were clear of danger, Pops took time to check Isaac over. "Are you ok?" he asked.

Isaac was wide-eyed, trembling, and had a hard time speaking. "What just happened?" was his confused response.

"You almost got taken out. That little mare almost got you for good." Pops said as he held him.

Isaac was starting to settle down and get his wits about him and he said again, "What happened? I didn't even see it coming, she just reared up and that's the last thing I knew. I wasn't being mean to her or nothin' so why did she do that?"

Pops then explained the entire event to him as he had seen it, then he asked, "Now do you understand why I told you kids to stay away from these mustangs? You didn't do anything wrong, they just aren't ready to be messed with yet."

"I understand better now why you told us that," Isaac replied. He was a little scraped up but luckily he was not seriously hurt. He was a fortunate boy and Pops was sure he was a little wiser too.

"Look there. After that horse attack your hat is still on your head. It's a good thing that you keep it pulled down so tight," Pops said, trying to distract him and ease his mind.

Isaac later related the experience to the rest of the family. "I don't really know what happened. I was just trying to be nice and pet the horse, and I wasn't going to hurt her or nothin'," he said with sincerity. "Just about the time I was going to pet her, all of a sudden she reared up and that's the last thing I remember until I was runnin' away from the mare and Dad came hurryin' to help me. It all happened so fast."

"Are you hurt anywhere?" Momma K inquired.

"I kind of feel sore and a little beat up and the back of my neck sort of hurts a little but I guess I was lucky to not be worse off. I'll think twice before I go up to the next horse that I don't know and I think I'll let Dad do it first. Then maybe I'll give it a try."

From then on, it wasn't just Pops warning everyone to be careful around the mustangs. Isaac also let them know to watch out. This obviously proved to be one of those close-call learning experiences for them all. Pops learned to use better horse training practices and be more careful about the type of horses that he brought around the family, and the kids learned to listen to Pops when he warned them to steer clear of potential trouble.

"Picket Fence"

"A Good Time to Pray"

"Kids—The Real Thing"

8. THE PINEVIEW ROUNDUP

Pops and Momma K, with the kids in tow, often drove from state to state traveling to art shows or picking up horses to train or—even better—delivering horses somewhere to be sold. On one such drive, Momma K listened to the kids talking as they watched out of the car windows.

She heard, "Hey there's one," as Isaac pointed out the window.

"That's bigger than the last one we saw," Levi remarked.

"Yeah but I like the white and red painted wooden ones better, even if it's not as big," Isaac added.

"But the metal ones are stronger and you don't get slivers in your hands when you climb over 'em," Levi said. They both nodded and said, "Yeah, that's right," in agreement.

Annie put in her two cents with, "I like the ones with the big tops over them. They're all shady and we can run up and down the stairs. And they have the treat places too."

It was then back to Levi who asked, "Dad, how come we don't have one in our town?"

In unison Isaac and Annie said, "Yeah how come? We should have one too!"

Cooper had been sleeping, but because of the commotion, he too began looking out the window to see what the talk was about.

He asked, "Is it a puppy? A pen of sheep? A pony? What are you all lookin' at?"

They drove the old Suburban along the outskirts of another western town which seemed to hold another clue as to what the kids were talking about, Momma K became curious herself. "What are you kids talking about?"

"You know those rodeo places?" Levi exclaimed.

It was then she realized exactly what they had been talking about. The small town arenas with their covered grandstands, the series of stock pens, bucking chutes, out buildings for housing a variety of livestock at County Fair time, and the concession stands where hot dogs, burgers, drinks, and treats are served.

Both Isaac and Levi reminded, "Yeah, remember the boots that we won for ridin' sheep in Colorado? Why don't we have sheep ridin' and rodeos in our town, Dad? Annie and Cooper want to win some boots too."

As they drove on, Pops reminisced with the kids of how it was when he was a young feller growing up in a small town. "Every Fourth of July a man named Vern Oyler with the 'Flyin' O' rodeo company would bring his travelin' miniature rodeo to the town square," Pops told them how they would set up the chutes, pens, and the net wire arena. Some of the local men from town would pitch in and help set it up. Using a tractor, they would spread tons of saw dust just outside the bucking chutes. "They did that to kind of protect the grass and keep the critters from slipping and falling," Pops said as he winked at the kids. "You all know the real reason? When we were little we didn't tend to ride near as good as you kids do. Most of us only made it two or three jumps and we were bucked off. That pile of saw dust made a nice soft landing." He continued,

"Anyway, on the big day, all of us kids would enter up and go to riding a jumpin', bawlin' calf or a buckin' pony."

Cooper piped up, "A pony! Where's a pony? I don't see one." They all chuckled. It was obvious what Cooper was always thinking about.

Pops went on, "Some of the kids would win little trophies and the rest of us kids would all get a ribbon for our efforts. My oldest brother won a lot of times. Once he and one of his buddies even rode a buckin' pony double, it was quite a show." It was fun for Pops to reflect and think of those days and share those times with the kids.

"Did you win, Dad?" one of them asked.

"I was kind of at the tail end of the whole era. Ol' Vern died and the little rodeo just kind of went away about the time I was old enough to really get involved. I was younger, pretty scared, and usually on my own. So if I entered and rode I never stayed on and sometimes, at the last minute, I even chickened out. Like I said, we weren't as good as you kids are," Pops added. "No matter what, it was always a great time and left me with a whole pile of good memories."

"How long has it been since the town had a rodeo?" Levi inquired.

"Oh it was twenty years or so," Pops guessed. "There will never be a rodeo as good as that one was," he said confidently.

All during the conversation, ambitious Momma K was listening, scheming, and going over an idea in her mind. One can see where

Cooper gets some of his ways. "Why don't we start our own?" She offered boldly.

"Our own what?" Pops questioned.

"Our own rodeo! It's obvious the only way to recreate that experience for these kids and others is for us to start our own rodeo company!" The kids were all jumping up and down cheering at the idea. They were obviously all in for the plan.

"That's crazy! You have no clue how big of a project that would be. We don't have chutes, portable fencing, or livestock, not to mention the insurance nightmare it would be," Pops said.

She said simply, "Well someone has that stuff, and we can find it, or figure out how to get it or make it ourselves. We could hire parts of the event out or rent some stuff or even get some things donated. Good people are always willing to support events for kids!"

Now the wheels were turning in her head and the encouragement from the excited kids was spurring her on. Pops thought to himself, here we go, I'd better hang on for this ride. Pops never did any good when he entered in the little rodeos of his youth. He could see that they were in for a wild ride now. He also knew with her enthusiasm it was going to be a good one.

"We'll help you! We wanna help," the kids all offered.

Once they got home Momma K was on the phone nonstop for the next couple of months. She formed a committee, got town approval, arranged for insurance, rounded up livestock, hired a for-real rodeo announcer, and a mountain of other things that had to be done in order to pull off one little Independence Day rodeo. At one point she realized the rodeo needed its own name. After many suggestions and discussions, they decided on "Pineview Roundup," named after a nearby lake. It just seemed to fit. They even made

T-shirts with a bucking pony and big letters that said "Pineview Roundup." It was a hit.

Coming up with an arena and building the chutes was left to Pops. He enlisted the help of many people to make it all come together. The day before the event, they set up the arena, chutes, and catch pens. A hay wagon with some bales of hay on it made a great announcer's stand. They dragged in the bleachers from the baseball diamond. It looked great, just like the real thing. The kids were so excited they got in the chutes, flung the gates open, and came barreling out as if they were on a wild bucking bull, practicing for the big day.

The time for the rodeo finally arrived. After the community breakfast, the parade, and the patriotic program, it was time to have some big fun. There were many other activities going on in the town square at the same time as the rodeo, so they were concerned that they wouldn't have any spectators at all.

At the last minute they were so busy with final preparations — filling the fishpond with water, sorting the animals, checking all the gates, placing hay bales and whatever else needed to be done, it was a little frantic. Then one of the kids tugged on Pops' sleeve. He glanced up to say, "What do you need Cheyenne? Can't you see that I'm busy right now?" With awe she said, "But Daddy, look at all of 'em."

"All of what?" Pops questioned.

"All the people!" she scolded.

Pops had been so busy that he hadn't even looked up to see that the stands were packed. Waiting spectators were sitting or standing on any open spot of grass they could find. Several hundred people were anticipating a great little rodeo.

"I guess we'd better put on a good show," Pops said as they hurried to finish up. The announcer welcomed the fans and the show was on. No one was disappointed because a great little rodeo is exactly what they had. "If you build it, they will come." There couldn't have been a truer statement.

The events were generally family-oriented. Momma K included a father and son hay bale rolling race around some obstacles. She even had a daddy daughter fish pond relay where they filled a several-hundred-gallon steel water trough and loaded it with gold fish. The teams would run across the arena. The dad had to get into the tank, catch some fish bare-handed, put them in a plastic bag, and hand it off to the waiting daughter. She would then race, squealing with joy, to the finish line.

The team-roping event got a little wild. An adult and a child teamed up on foot to head and heel a small steer. Usually a dad would rope the head and try with all his macho might to hold it while the youngster would attempt to get a rope on the hind feet of the critter. All grass-stained and rope-burned, the teams would limp out of the arena smiling and relishing the fun time they had. Mostly it was the dads who went in the arena to help the kids with the dirty work, while the mothers were content to watch and cheer from the sidelines.

One of the crowd's favorite events was the wild calf dressing.

Once again the macho men were sure to win! The event started out with a group of calves turned out into the arena as several two-person teams sprang from the opposite side of the arena with the excitement of ready, set, go! The goal was to simply put a T-shirt on your chosen calf, over its head with the two front legs through the armholes of the shirt. As it should be, a team of two seasoned mothers won the race almost before it started. It was a couple of sisters who had been raised on a dairy farm. They had bottle fed hundreds of calves and one had several wild kids of her own that she had dressed in a similar fashion for years. The girls had an obvious unfair advantage. They made it fun to watch.

They had calf riding and then the sheep riding. Pops pulled out the secret weapon— Annie's patented and proven style of backwards mutton bustin'. She was again the star of the show. The style caught on and many other kids perfected it too.

Levi and Isaac dressed up as rodeo clowns complete with raggedy old clothes and painted faces. Along with a couple of their friends, they ran around helping the younger kids and just generally showing off and having fun. Everyone had a great time and all the kids got tasty candy prizes.

Later that evening after the dust had settled, the crowds had gone, and the portable arena was taken down, Pops, Momma K, and the kids laid on the soft grass. They were looking up into the sky waiting for the fireworks to start and create the big finale to the festivities of the day when one of the kids asked, "Dad, was that rodeo as good as when you were a kid?"

As Pops lay there, sore and exhausted, he responded with, "Either my memory is fadin' or that was the best rodeo I've ever been to. Was it fun for you?"

"It was the best, Dad," they all agreed. "Can we do it again?"

"We'll have to see if Mom is up to it," Pops winked at Momma K.

They did it again year after year.

She put in countless hours on this ambitious undertaking, organizing volunteers, working with the town council, finding new help, and prizes for the kids, more stock, and designing new events. She was always riding hard and in the eyes of the many happy rodeo kids Momma K was riding tall. She loved them and they loved her.

"She was Riding Tall"

"Kids—Sure Enough the Real Thing"

9. He's a Dandy

With another summer winding down, Fall was fast approaching. The morning air was becoming crisp and the leaves were making their annual change from green to warm reds and oranges. It was time for the annual "Balloon Festival," a three-day event held in a large open park. The whole affair had the feel of an old-time circus coming to town. Thirty or so pilots with their hot air balloons would travel from near and far to participate.

The balloons came in a rainbow of colors and were covered with lively geometric patterns. Most were the traditional upside-down pear shape, but some were quite creative, like a frog, a fish, and even a giant stuffed bear shape. The balloons would hover around the valley and over the lake for hours. As the balloons would cool, they'd drift toward the earth. Then a fiery blast from their propane burners would roar like the breath of a fire-breathing dragon, and up into the sky they'd go again.

The grassy infield of the park would be packed with people and barefooted kids running here and there. The borders of the park hosted games, food venders, and stages for live entertainment. The air was filled with the tantalizing smells of honey-roasted almonds, popcorn, snow cones, cotton candy, watermelon, and all sorts of confections. For a kid, the excitement could be delirious. There was an antique car show, an art show, a small rodeo, a fishpond, a dunking machine, and several more games and booths filled with wares that people were peddling, but best of all, according to Cooper, there were pony rides.

"Under God's Thumbnail"

The main reason for Pops attending the festival was the art show. He'd go with high hopes of selling paintings to those in the crowd and he usually had pretty good luck. When a group of balloons were ready to ascend the loud speakers would play "Up, Up and Away." One time when Pops was setting up his art booth and "Up, Up and Away" started playing, he heard someone call to him from high overhead, "Daddy, look up here!" As he looked up, he thought to himself, that sounds like Annie, where could she be?

"Daddy! Look at us!" Then he saw her. She was calling from one of the hovering balloons. She and a cousin had been roaming the park as the balloons were being inflated. One crew was short-handed so the two of them pitched in to help. Consequently, they got invited to take a balloon ride. Pops waved and cautioned them to be careful (that was late advice) but it was fun to see her up there taking in the festivities.

The rest of the family had other motives to be there. Roaming the park, they'd take in all the sights, visit with friends, and eat more than their share of candy and treats. Even though Cooper would get lost in the crowds, Momma K didn't worry too much because she knew where he could eventually be found. Each time he came up missing, he would magically drift to the street, north of the park, where the pony rides were going on. Once he had been located, Momma K would say, "Coop, you can't wander off like that. You'll get lost."

He would respond with the innocent logic of a trusting eight-year-old, "But, Mom, I knew where I was the whole time, so I couldn't be lost."

How could she reason with that?

On this particular year, a lady named Rosie was in charge of the pony rides. She had one Shetland pony named Dandy that was of special interest to Cooper. Shetland ponies get their name from a set of islands near England, where they originally came from. They tend to be sturdy little things, not very big—about the size of a really big dog or about thigh-high to a man.

The minute Coop saw Dandy, he got very excited because standing right there in front of him was the pony of his dreams! Love at first sight! Dandy was a caramel bay color with a long, flowing,

flaxen mane and tail, and kind, gentle, lash-laden eyes. Best of all, according to Cooper, he was the perfect size for a little pony-lovin' boy. It only cost one dollar per pony ride but after all the other festival attractions, Cooper was too short of money to have a turn.

Cooper made a deal with Rosie that couldn't be refused. He offered to lead Dandy up and down the street while the paying kids had their rides. He didn't ask for anything in return for his "help," he just wanted to be near that pony. How could Rosie refuse? Over the next two days, Coop wore the leather off the soles of his boots. He walked up and down and up and down the street, hour after hour, from early in the morning 'til long after dark, just to hang with Dandy.

In visiting with Rosie, Cooper learned that Dandy had been Rosie's son's pony, but her son had grown too tall to ride him anymore. The Shetland had also been part of a wagon team but, sadly, during the previous winter, his harness-mate had gone to the Big Ranch.

Rosie was mighty impressed with Cooper's dedication and his affection for Dandy. She realized that, at her place, Dandy no longer had a buddy to keep him company, and she wanted more than anything for Dandy to have a good home. She quickly became sentimental about seeing Dandy and Cooper together. After the festival, she cautiously approached Pops and Momma K and offered to sell the pony to them. She was asking $1,000 for the pony and his cart. It was not an outrageous price, but it was a lot of money for a little feller like Coop to come up with. Considering the costs and still not being completely convinced about the idea of having a pony around, Pops said, "If Cooper can come up with the money, on his own, he can have him." He was, of course, fairly confident that Cooper would have a tough time coming up with that much money.

A wise person never underestimates the power in a pint. And the cork on this one was about to explode at the prospect of having his own pony, the one from his dreams. Cooper had never been more focused on anything than he was about buying this pony. He decided right then and there that he was going to somehow earn the money. After all, he had finally found the exact pony he'd dreamed of and Pops appeared to be softening to the idea of letting him have one.

Rosie must have sensed what was in the air because she said, "Hey, I'm going out of town right after the festival. Would it be alright if Cooper took care of Dandy while I'm away? Then we can see if these two can get along for real." Pops reluctantly agreed. So the next day, Rosie delivered Dandy.

A few days later at about midday, Momma K watched as Cooper and Annie trotted out the driveway with Dandy hitched to the pony cart.

"Where are they going?" Momma K asked Pops.

"I am not sure, but I think they'll be fine. I'm sure they'll be back soon. They can't be going too far with those short little legs pulling them." Or so he thought.

The pony cart was a lightweight rig that rode on two bicycle wheels with a padded, coil-spring seat that could easily accommodate three small passengers. Two shafts extended from the cart and

ran up either side of the pony, attaching to the harness through a series of buckles, rings, and straps. As the pony trotted, the passengers experienced the full effect of the short rhythmic jolting motions of his gait. The faster the pony trotted, the more the jolting and bouncing. The more the bouncing, the bigger the smiles. As was bound to happen, those smiles soon turned into uncontrolled giggles and there was happiness all over the place. When there is enough jolting, bouncing, smiling, and giggling, kids really can't help but be having a whole cartload of fun.

Annie had made a sack lunch for them, which they had stowed carefully in the cart. Several hours later, Momma K got concerned, wondering where the trio was and if they were okay. When she couldn't take it any longer, she went looking for them. She found the crew only a few blocks away from home. They had discovered a birthday party going on so they made themselves conveniently available to give cart rides to all the kids who were there. By the time Momma K found them, Dandy was unharnessed and tied to a fence. Coop and Annie were caught up in the middle of a bunch of balloons and party-hat clad kids, thoroughly enjoying the festivities. Dandy was munching on the overgrown grass along the fence line while the kids enjoyed cake and ice cream. She found that they were more than just okay. Not wanting to appear overly concerned she asked, "Whatchya been doin' kids?"

"We've been working, Mom," they piped up. Annie filled her in, "We were just trottin' along and saw all these kids playin' in this yard. They waved to us and some came running out to the road and asked if they could have a ride or if they could pet Dandy."

"Then what?"

"Well, Cooper didn't even flinch. He said for a dollar we'll give you a ride." And they all just lined up, moms and kids alike, so we gave a bunch of rides. I collected the money and Cooper just kept makin' trips around the block, kid after kid."

"Cooper, do you feel good about that?" Momma K asked.

"I sure do! This is fun. We get cake, all the kids are happy, and we get paid. It don't get any better than that."

Cake and ice cream couldn't compete,
With his pony hitched to the cart.
Kids lined up for a turn on the seat,
And giggles came straight from the heart.

Coop had $60 in his pocket from generous parents of the partygoers and they had more treats than they could eat. Cooper felt like he was well on his way toward earning the money that he needed. Like Pops said, he was a determined little pint. Momma K was pleased with her little business kids and left them to their own devices.

With a little help, Cooper placed an advertisement in the local newspaper offering to hire out, providing pony cart rides for birthday parties and other events. With the cart being able to carry two or three kids at the same time, and with his being able to ride instead of walk, he could go all day and make more money besides. Cooper had never been a bashful boy, and he had a way with people. He was able to put on a fair show, even stopping to play "Happy Birthday" or some other simple tune on his fiddle. He was a hit and word of his gig spread fast. Cooper and Dandy also frequented the local park on the lookout for picnickers. Annie helped him make a sign that they hung on the side of the cart. It read, "RIDES $1.00." Every kid that passed would go crazy and Coop would be busy for a couple of hours. Many times he returned home, beaming with bulging pockets.

Coop also found other sources of income. He wrangled a job feeding horses for Kristie. She lived at Horse Creek Ranch in Wyoming, but she had a pasture close to Pop's place where she kept some horses year round. He rustled up other odd jobs around the community to help raise the funds he needed.

For Christmas that year, Isaac, with the help of a neighbor and some abandoned snowmobile skis, rigged up sleigh runners for the pony cart. Cooper would park at the town ice skating rink, selling rides to those who had ventured out into the cold. At the end of a long, cold season of feeding horses, giving sleigh rides, and counting his pennies, Cooper had almost saved up enough money to pay for Dandy and the cart. Pops was cornered and he could not go back on the deal.

As his money pile grew, Cooper became more and more creative and motivated to make the deal complete. All growing up Cooper had heard the sagey phrase from Grandpa Eddy, "There's nothin' better for the inside of a man than the outside of a horse." Unconsciously, he figured that it must apply to little boys too because having Dandy had made him take on the drive and responsibilities of a real man. Pops and Momma K couldn't have been more proud.

The day finally came. Coop had put together all the money he needed to pay Rosie. Pops drove him to her house. Coop knocked on the door and she answered. He reached out his little arm and handed her an envelope full of cash and said, "Here it is. You can count it if you want, it's all there. Thanks for selling me Dandy. I like him a lot."

With tears in her eyes, she accepted the money. Instead of counting it, she just wrapped Coop in a big hug and thanked him too. She was very happy that Dandy had a good home and was proud of Cooper's ambition.

With the business deal complete, Dandy was all his own and he was sure enough riding tall. It's true, "There's nothin' better for the inside of a boy than the outside of a pony."

"Sir Coopalot"

10. SIR COOPALOT

His pony and he could be a mighty fine sight,
In a WILD WEST Bill Cody show.
He'd save a fair maiden from the Black Knight,
While slayin' dragons in the full moon's glow.

Cowboy songs on the radio and the many western movies he watched carried Cooper to faraway ranges covered with sweet-smelling sage, cactus flowers, fleeting antelope, roaming buffalo, and many hidden surprises. There were endless destinations in his well-traveled mind—a source of dreams that never seemed to rest.

Along with his cow-punching fantasies, Coop had a growing fascination with medieval horsemen. He dreamed about dragon-slaying, armored knights with their fawning fair maidens, and King Arthur and his supposed pal, Sir Lancelot. As he read stories with Momma K and watched movies about these heroic characters, he could imagine himself on a mighty jousting horse, fighting opposing knights with a lance and a gleaming sword, all while crowds of spectators looked on.

As Pops had learned, when Cooper gets something boiling in his hot little head, one can almost see the steam of ambition whistling out his ears. Pops knew something was up when the boy asked if he could have an old garbage can lid—one that had outlived the can it belonged to. It would make a great shield. The lid was just the right shape and size and it even had a handle in the middle to hang onto. An oil funnel from the shop, dressed up with red shoofly tassels off of a driving bridle, made a handsome knight's helmet. Baseball catcher shin guards made convincing leg armor.

Pops asked Cooper "What are you doing?" He responded only with, "Oh nothin'. You'll see when I'm done," sounding as only a confident ten-year-old can. You know, one that regularly claims, "I am the boss of myself," and is always in charge.

With a pair of Pop's old welding gloves, an old wool plaid jacket, and miscellaneous colorful scarves, feathers, and plumes, he was prepared for both battle and conquest. It was obvious that Coop would soon need to be outfitting his steed. Sure enough, the request came. He ran to Momma K and asked, "Mom, I need to make armor for Dandy. Do you have some shiny metal I can use?"

She replied (straight faced, bless her), "No, but I am sure we can think of something else that will work just as well."

He nodded an "Okay" and went back to work. Arming this young knight's mount looked like it would be more complicated than outfitting the knight had been. But he fixed his mind on the task and set out to get it done. He rummaged through some old linen in the closet and found an outdated, green, ribbed bedspread—the kind a person might find at a cheap motel or covering a well-worn sofa in a grandma's house.

"Mom, can I use this old thing?" He hollered from the back room. After much pleading from the very determined would-be knight and the lofty promise that a certain room would be kept clean, he was allowed to have his way with the blanket. He asked for scissors, shoestrings, and a handful of safety pins. Then he disappeared to the barnyard for more than two hours. When Sir Coopalot finally returned to the house, it was raining, and the family was treated to one of the most curious sights imaginable. The results of Cooper's handiwork would have made any seamstress proud.

He had rigged Dandy with the old high-backed saddle that had been handed down from Grandpa Eddy. The green bedspread was then draped over Dandy's entire body from head to tail. He had cut two eyeholes and two slots for Dandy's ears, and then he put a bridle on him, which helped to keep the drape over his head secured and hold it in place. The area over the saddle had then been tailored with a hole for the horn to poke through and another for the high cantle. This slight modification helped to keep the rest of the bedspread in its proper place. The last strategic cuts

were notches to expose the rounded and worn oxbow stirrups of the antique saddle. The handful of safety pins and shoelaces were clasped and woven under Dandy's neck and tail to tie up the loose ends of the bedspread.

Dandy's soft, whiskered muzzle peeked out the front end and his two long-lashed, shiny eyes peered through the jagged holes in the cloth, along with protruding strands of his long, shaggy forelock.

His stubby ears poked out their provided openings and hints of his generous and unruly mane could be seen under his neck. His chunky pony form was recognizable beneath the drape and his tiny feet were exposed to his ankles. Last but not least, by any knight's standards, his long flaxen tail flowed freely from the other end of the bedspread.

When the other kids saw Coop's renaissance masterpiece they applauded him. But Annie was a little sore. "Why didn't you tell me you were makin' a costume for you and Dandy? I would have wanted to help," she scolded. "You know I could've helped you and it would've been even neater."

"Sorry Annie, I was in too big of a hurry to ask for any help. I needed to get the knight stuff put together because I had knight stuff to do. You can help next time," Cooper replied.

Never in all medieval countryside or fairytale land was there ever a finer looking or better outfitted jousting steed to be found. Momma K marveled as the fearless knight and his mighty steed charged up and down the pasture again and again. Dandy's little feet were only a blur. His nostrils flared and his tail flew straight out behind him. Cooper, like a caped crusader, slashed the air with his wooden sword and thrust forward the broken shovel handle that served as a jousting lance.

Coop dressed himself and his pony up like this many times, and every conquest to save a fair maiden or slay a troublesome dragon or rid the pasture of Orcs was a fabulous adventure. These crusades went on for several weeks. The day they put that old bedspread to rest was a sad one. Pops was looking out the window of the back door when Cooper came to the house. His little shoulders were drooping and shaking in time with his audible sobs. In his hands he grasped a mass of soaking wet green rags, spotted with mud and showing the glint of the occasional crippled safety pin. When Pops asked what had happened, Coop blurted out, "We were goin' through the river and Dandy put his head down to drink and he stepped on it!"

In his mind, Pops could see how the deed had been done. Dandy had stepped on a corner of the flowing drapery as it floated on the water's surface and when he attempted to raise his head out of the water and couldn't, he panicked, bolted, and ran right through the bedspread, leaving the drape in shreds and the little knight red-faced and tear stained. Pops spared the knight his honor as he smiled inside, repressing a chuckle as he imagined the comical scene that it must have been.

The dejected little knight's grief was soon chased away with some gentle, understanding words from Momma K, the offer of homemade cookies, and a big glass of cool milk. He was soon feeling better enough to get to scheming and planning his next adventure.

"The Headless Horseman"

"Saddle Buds"

11. ROUND 'EM UP

"When's it gonna be time for Fall round up?" Levi and Isaac anxiously asked Pops.

Preoccupied in whatever "important" thing he was doing, and without looking up, he simply answered, "That's a silly question. In the Fall of course."

"No Dad, you know what we mean," they complained.

"I'm just messin' with you. Everyone will be gathering soon. But you don't really want to go help this year, do you?" Pops teased.

"Who's askin' the silly question now? You know we do, we're always ready to gather cattle," they protested.

Cooper chimed in, "Me too! I am, too!"

Isaac poked him in the ribs and quipped, "You can't go with us. Your pony is too little to be any good on cows. You won't be able to keep up. You've gotta ride big horses like us to do any good."

To Cooper, those were fightin' words. "Dandy is too good. You don't know, we can do anything you can do and I am goin'." He turned to Pops and asked (or claimed was more like it), "I can go can't I, Pops?"

"Well you are pretty handy on old Dandy, but I don't know if you are ready for roundup. We'll have to see what your Mother says about it."

Cooper had many ambitions, but most of all he wanted to be a cowboy. Because cowboyin' was all about fun. Going with the "big boys" to help in the roundup was just another one of Coop's dreams. The discussion was dropped for the time being and plans were made so they'd be ready when the calls started coming in.

Pops, Momma K, and Cooper had a long discussion about the idea of Coop joining the big boys on the next roundup. It was finally decided that if he would follow directions and not get in the way, he would be allowed to go along.

Fall roundups are always looked forward to. Along with them being a reunion of sorts for the older people, it's also a proving ground for the younger fellers, the up-and-coming cowboys. It's hard work, but for a cowboy that type of work is fun.

During the annual event, cattle are gathered from the summer ranges, sorted, checked for sickness, culled, and counted. The calves are weaned from the mother cows and shipped to market. The rest are then put into winter feed lots. "The Gather" typically means cold early mornings, long hot days, and miles and miles of riding up hills, down hills, and through washes, canyons, and draws. Mosquitoes, horse flies, chiggers, no see'ums, and ticks are a herder's most faithful traveling companions. Cowboys must endure dusty choking trails, muddy rain-saturated slickers, stinky wet socks, and sweat-soaked hats—all for the honor and privilege of trailing the south end of a northbound, smelly old cow. Again, "It's all about havin' fun."

Sometimes moving cows is sort of like trying to push a soft string. For some reason, cattle like going uphill when a cowboy wants them to go down, but when he needs them to go down, they would rather go up. Mostly they just like hiding deep in the scrub oak, hawthorn, and maple bushes—brush so thick that a cowboy can't even see through it. You can be moving ten-head of wily first-calf heifers, a couple of old cow-calf pairs, and a rangy bull toward the holding corrals and if the critters got a chance, they'd disappear into the edge of a thicket like cool milk soaking into hot chocolate cake. They never even leave a trace. Some cowboys attempt to venture into the thicket after them, but more often than not they are forced to retreat covered with scratches, thorn pricks, bruises, and burrs. They might be holding a couple of broken saddle strings and missing their hat or at the least it's been reshaped by some low-hanging branch.

Of course the part that would always make the day complete for Pops was when Cheyenne and Momma K would meet the boys at noonday. Annie loved to look after her boys. "My guys," she would say. "I need to get some treats for my guys."

Momma K and Annie would drive the truck and meet the boys somewhere on

the trail with a picnic lunch and there'd be plenty of treats for their guys. They'd tie the horses and spread a blanket on the ground. Taking a break, they'd likely tell some ever-expanding buckaroo stories, some that had got their start only just that morning.

Once they were stuffed with treats and the horses watered, it was time to get back to work. Saddles were retightened, gear was checked, and the Wild Bunch remounted. "Thanks for the lunch, Mom. You too, Annie," Pops and the boys would say.

Many times, cautions had been offered by well-meaning people. Things like, "Those kids are too small to help with the cattle," or "It's just not safe." But Pops was glad they weren't heeded because he would hate to think of all the great times they would have missed out on. Pops never rode more, or more proud, than when he and the boys were working cattle or doing other things together as a family.

"Hey boys, I got a call they're gathering the old Wangsgard range next Saturday. Are you ready to go?" Pops asked. Like he didn't know what the answer would be.

"You bet we are." Levi and Isaac were all in.

"So am I," Coop reminded.

"Who said he could go?" Levi protested.

"Mom and I talked it over and we decided that it would be ok if he came along this year. Besides, you kids started goin' about his age so we think it's time for him to go and he promised that he would mind and stay out of the way."

"But he don't even ride a big horse." Isaac argued.

"It'll be fine. You'll see. We can all help look out for him. Ok?" Pops' word was final. But he did keep his fingers crossed that all would go well.

The day came and the gather was going well. Everyone was doing their part and more. So far, Cooper had minded well and stayed clear of trouble most of the morning. Later there was an event, or in other words, a growing experience. But with Cooper along that should have been expected.

For the next few months, Pops found himself recounting the event to his friends. Pops would explain, "It was late in the morning and me and Coop were pushin' a group of cattle when they dove into a thicket of oak brush without leaving a trace as to where they went. Undaunted, that little feller on his little pony and with old Belle at his side ducked into the brush right behind those cattle." Pops would lean back as he went on, "Coop was making a bunch of noise, he was a whoopin' and hollerin', talkin' to the cattle, along with the sounds of him crashing through the brush. And that old dog was barkin' and branches were breakin'. I think they left a mark in the brush where those cattle hadn't."

Pops continued, "I was stopped dead in my tracks by those low-hanging branches. I wasn't any help at all. I called after him, 'Hey, don't you go in there! Can't you hear me? I said don't go in there!'

But I realized it was no use. He was determined and well on his way, so I changed my tune. I started coaching him from outside the brush. 'You be careful. Watch out for that bull. Make sure he don't turn back on you,' I told him. I don't remember what all I said and I wasn't sure if he was even hearin' me. I'd holler, 'Can you hear me?' and all I'd get back was, 'Whoop, whoop, get up cow, come on move you old cows.'"

Pops was proud, but not too braggy. He'd go on, "Then like too much milk oozing out the other side of the chocolate cake, here they come. Just like they'd known all along exactly what they were doin'. The noisy trio and the mob of cattle emerged from the opposite side of the thicket and without a scratch, and those cattle were travelin' single file, heads hangin' down, and headed straight toward the corrals. Cooper had even kept the old bull moving, which sure looked annoyed but he was moving in the right direction."

From then on when a stubborn bunch of critters got in brush too thick for the big boys, it was Cooper and Dandy to the rescue.

Against his original claims about the usefulness of ponies, Pops was often found bragging about the willingness and ambition of Cooper and Dandy when moving those cattle. Sometimes he would shamelessly claim, "I knew all along that little pony would come in good for somethin'. He was sure 'nuff handy, Dandy."

Cooper was mighty proud to be whooping and hollering, and saving the day, despite the bruises, eating dust, and getting bug bites. You know, he was just riding tall and having fun.

"Endangered Species"

Cooper riding Duke, leading pack mule

12. BIGGER PONIES

Over the next couple of years, Cooper and Dandy proved their worth time after time. As roundups came and went, Cooper was naturally growing taller. As he got bigger, he was more able to handle larger and unfamiliar ponies. This also meant he was more helpful when it came to training for other people.

Dr. John had purchased a couple of young Welsh ponies and he needed them trained so he came calling. Pops and the boys were happy to help him. Welsh ponies are a little larger than Shetland ponies. Dr. John bought them from the Garden of Eden Pony Farm. Now that is a place Cooper liked to visit. They had many fancy ponies, all registered with unusual names like Charlemagne or Sinbad. Some even had four or five names. As an experiment in making an even larger and more unique pony breed, they had crossed many of them with Arabian stallions. This cross tended to make them hot-blooded and a real handful to train.

The Garden of Eden farm was a pretty site, roughly 320 acres of meadows, hay fields, and cottonwood-filled river bottoms. The bottoms were shady and cool and many of the big trees were topped with large nests that eagles and red-tailed hawks called home. There were foxes, badgers, rock chucks, pot gut squirrels, and a large band of mule deer meandering and moving about. A little old farmhouse, built in the 1880s, sat neatly on a bluff overlooking it all. A stone's throw away was a barn with a huge hayloft which hosted a family of great horned owls. The loft was a young explorer's paradise, hay bales could be rearranged to become imaginary forts and places to hide and play. Two rows of box stalls had automatic water troughs and feed mangers positioned beneath openings in the ceiling so feed could be dropped down from the loft above. The buildings were fire engine red with white trim. Tree lined lanes and rail fences separated the yards from pastures. A real ranch.

The ponies that Dr. John purchased and brought to be trained were full brothers and black as coal. Romeo had a white star mark on his forehead, but Licorice was solid black from nose to tail. These ponies were three and four years old and hadn't been handled much, so they were both hotter than a pistol. Through methodical gentling and a couple months of careful, yet intense riding, they became trustable for most anyone to ride. Cooper didn't mind working long hours with the ponies. He would find his way into the house, tired yet happy after a big day of training. "These ponies of

Dr. John's sure are fast," he'd regularly say. He was having a hard time admitting it, but he was starting to like the bigger and faster mounts because he was getting bigger and faster himself.

While Romeo and Licorice were at the place, Dandy was put out to pasture. One can't help but think he enjoyed the rest. When the black ponies were sent back to Doctor John's, trained to a tee, it was time to get back to his ol' pal Dandy.

"How did you like riding those bigger ponies?" Pops asked.

Without hesitation, Coop replied, "I liked it fine but Dandy and me have some catchin' up to do, we gotta team up."

"What do you mean by team up?" Pops wasn't sure what he had in mind, but he soon found out.

When it comes to cowboyin', most everyone has heard of Team Ropin', but not too many have heard of Team Fishin'. When the water would rise high in Spring Creek and flood the grassy banks, it meant that it was time for Cooper and Dandy to do some Team Fishing. Coop liked to fish from Dandy's back. They were quite a team. Dandy was steady and willing to venture into deep water while Cooper, with his bow ready, kept his scouting eyes peeled for boiling schools of fish. On a hot afternoon in the shallows of the flooded river, they could easily haul in twenty to thirty stinky carp. They'd leave the catch on the bank for the foxes and wild cats to eat. When he and Dandy returned the following day, the  fish would be all gone and they could resume their Team Fishing. It became a favorite after-school activity.

After one particularly good day of fishing, Coop came home to a ringing phone. "Hello. Yeah, this is Cooper. Who is this?" A silent pause as he listened intently. "Oh yeah, sure I'll do that. When do you want to bring 'em? Ok I'll talk to my Dad and he'll call you. Thanks for callin.'"

Momma K was close by and overheard the conversation—well at least one side of it. "Who was that?" She asked.

Coop replied, "It was Mrs. Yeager."

"Mrs. Yeager from the Garden of Eden Pony Farm?" she confirmed. "What did she want?"

"She wants me to train a couple of ponies for her," Coop replied as he swaggered out of the room. "I guess she heard how good of a job I did on Dr. John's ponies so she wants to hire me to ride some for her," he casually made known to all within earshot.

Whether it is for the good or for the bad, word gets around in a small town.

Mrs. Yeager had learned what a good job Cooper had done with Dr. John's black ponies. Arrangements were made and she brought two more ponies for Cooper to ride. The first was a bally-faced, stocking-legged bay named Flashlight. He was seven years old and had been green-broke a few years earlier, but hadn't been ridden since. Mrs. Yeager wanted the pony ridden and tuned up because he was to be a present for a little girl named Olivia the following Christmas.

With a gleam in her eye, Mrs. Yeager pulled Coop aside and said, "Now Cooper, I need your help. I know that you play with Olivia a lot but you have to keep Flashlight a secret from her. We don't want to spoil her Christmas surprise, do we?" While he was working it over in his mind she said, "Can you do that for us?"

He declared, "It sounds hard, but I'll sure try." This was going to be especially difficult because Olivia only lived a block away and Coop saw her most every day.

Olivia was a precocious little girl, just two years younger than Cooper. She had wide, lash-laden hazel eyes. Her long, dark hair hung clear to her waist in perfect ringlets that bounced along with her secure way of going. She was happy and she always had encouraging things to say to everyone she met, speaking with words and a manner well beyond her years. It was easy to see why Cooper liked to play with her and take her for pony cart rides. Their frequent association was going to make it difficult to maintain the secret. He had his work cut out for him.

"Buffalo Girl"

The other pony Mrs. Yeager brought was a fancy black roan named Blue Eclipse. He had one piercing, crystal-clear blue eye. In a horse, an eye like that is known as a "glass eye" because it looks just like a pretty, transparent glass marble. Blue Eclipse was two years old, a full brother to Romeo and Licorice, and just as fiery. He actually made Coop a little nervous to work with at first. With Pops' help, the same patient process was applied as had been done with Blue's brothers. Once the roan was coming along, accepting a rider and responding to training, Pops backed off and Coop continued to work the ponies himself every day for the next month. The bay was a piece of cake to work with, he was quickly tuned up and ready to go. Flashlight was bound to be a great Christmas surprise for Olivia.

The roan took more time, but he was learning well and becoming more and more comfortable around people. Cooper was starting to connect with him. Sadly, it all came perfectly together as he was finished working with him. Coop was going to miss Blue. It was likely he'd never see the pony again, because now that he was started he would be sold once he was returned to the farm. The ponies were returned to the Garden of Eden. Mrs. Yeager was satisfied with the job that he had done and she paid Cooper well.

Once she had loaded the ponies in her trailer and was about to leave, she said to Cooper, "How did we do on keeping Flashlight a secret from Olivia?"

"I did my best. She saw me riding him a time or two, but I never let on that it had anythin' to do with her. She sure liked the looks of him. When I'd ride by her yard she'd say somethin' like 'That sure is a cute pony, Cooper' or 'I really like his stocking legs.' I made sure that I didn't say anythin' about him maybe bein' a present for her. I don't think she has a clue, it is going to be a big surprise for her,"

Cooper was all too happy to say.

"Good work. I have a feelin' that we will do business again." They shook on it and she left him there to dream. He was thinking about bigger ponies. Did he want one?

He thought to himself, I sure like ridin' that little roan. I could make him into a good cowpony one day. It would be a lucky kid that got him for a Christmas surprise.

Cooper, Olivia and Dandy

"Four Friends"

13. THE DREAM DEAL

When Mrs. Yeager's ponies left, Cooper was back to riding his old pal Dandy again. Dandy was always willing and ready for any adventure and Cooper had strong feelings for him, but Coop was growing taller and getting bigger while Dandy wasn't. As time went on, he started thinking about those Welsh ponies he'd trained and how they had fit him so well and he liked that.

Cooper even considered the painful idea of selling Dandy. He really wanted a bigger pony and he also wanted to keep Dandy, "Have his chocolate cake and eat it too." But he knew Pops would not go for that. It had taken forever and been hard enough talking him into one pony, so two was surely out of the question. The idea of Dandy leaving hurt too much, it was almost more than he could take. Coop was tortured by his pony dilemma.

In talking to Cooper, Kristie from Horse Creek Ranch learned of the decision he was wrestling with. She knew how he felt about Dandy, so she came up with the perfect solution and offered it to Cooper. "Cooper, maybe I could help you and you could help me at the same time."

"What do you mean?" he said.

"Well I could buy Dandy from you. You know that I have always adored him. Right now my grandkids aren't big enough to ride him, but one day they will be. So you could keep him here until I'm ready for him."

"That sounds like a pretty good deal to me," he responded.

"In addition to that, I'd like to hire you to keep him in good shape and keep him fed for me in the winter."

"That sounds way good! Let's shake on it!"

Not even Pops could argue with this offer. Cooper was dancing on clouds at the prospect of getting a bigger pony and Dandy still being close by.

"Shadow Play"

When the deal was done, Pops and Momma K thanked Kristie for her generosity. She replied with a piece of wisdom she had learned from an old horse trader who worked for the Lazy Two Ranch. "If we agree to trade two $400 cats for one $800 dog, it's okay," she said. "It doesn't matter what the cats and dog may be worth to anyone else, just so long as both of us are happy with the deal." Kristie assured them, "And I couldn't be happier with having Dandy for my grandkids someday. I intend to keep him for a good long time. I feel like that pony is worth every bit I paid for him. So if Cooper is happy, I'm happy. It's a great deal, so thanks to all of you."

Once the deal was official, Cooper wanted to take Dandy for one last outing to a special place they liked to go. Over the years, Coop

"Every Kid's Dream"

and his brothers had built a camping spot along Spring Creek in some willow trees a mile or so from the house. Using hay strings and odd pieces of rope to lash together driftwood and branches they had dragged up from the river, the boys had built a small corral. With the same type of materials, they had built a little table and a lean-to for shade. With large river rocks, they had formed a good-sized ring to contain a campfire. During the construction process, the kids would be gone for hours on end. Then they'd return home long enough to get some food, stuff it in their saddle bags, crawl back on their horses, and head back to their campsite.

"Coop," his mom suggested on more than one occasion, "Why don't you just eat here? It would be so much easier."

"I can't," he would explain, "Mountain men and cowboys don't always come home to eat."

After the campsite was completed, Cooper asked Pops if he could stay there overnight. Pops thought it was a great idea, an adventure every boy should have. Momma K, on the other hand, imagined the bears and wolves waiting to eat him, so she did not like the plan at all. Coop and Pops banded together and won out, and Coop got his camping things together. He packed everything he thought he would need including, of course, plenty of treats and munchies. Then his mother equipped him with a walkie-talkie, just in case. She fought every impulse to check in at regular 15 minute intervals. Instead, she simply wished Cooper a good night and placed her walkie-talkie on the table by the bed.

Even for his young age, Coop had camped out many times, but this time proved to be different. It was a fairly cold and very dark night filled with what seemed an unusual amount of unidentifiable sounds. Or maybe it was the effect of the many treats that he had consumed just before he attempted to go to sleep. Whatever the boy-on-an-adventure reason was, every half hour or so, the walkie-talkie next to the bed produced a distant, scratchy little voice saying, "Mom, are you awake?" or "Mom, are you there?"

She would sleepily respond, "Sure, what do you need, honey?" or "Is everything okay?"

And Cooper would say, "Mom, what time is it?" or "I just can't sleep" or "I need more wood for the fire."

Finally, about four in the morning after countless unsuccessful attempts to doze, Momma K and Pops got out of bed. They left the rest of the kids sleeping cozily in their beds and went to Coop's rescue. They loaded up all the camping gear that had taken him several trips to haul down to the camp. By the time they got home, they were soaking wet from the dew-covered meadow grasses that lined the trail and wide awake. So instead of going straight to bed, they made waffles and hot chocolate, Coop's favorite. Then all three of them crawled into bed together, snuggled up, and finally got some sleep. What started out to be a miserable night ended up being a cherished bonding experience for them all.

> *Lay back in the grass on the bank of a brook*
> *Where dreams and reality tend to collide.*
> *Imagine cloud ponies as they softly drift by*
> *And remember the Dandy that you had to ride.*

Dandy stayed in a pasture owned by Horse Creek Ranch, for the next couple of years. It just happened to share the fence line with Pops' place. So Cooper could easily take good care of him. It was definitely a dream deal because the pain of parting with your first best friend can be terrible, so doing it slowly made it much less painful for Coop. Ultimately, Dandy moved clear across the country to Virginia where he lived out the rest of his life offering great pony adventures to Kristie's grandkids, just as he had done for Cooper.

Annie and Rusty

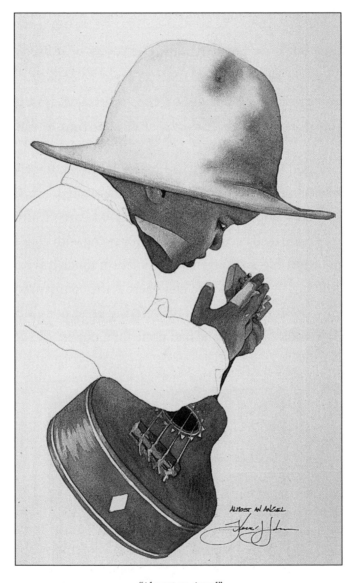

"Almost an Angel"

14. BANJO RETUNED

It seems that someone was always watching out for Coop—maybe the Cowboss and those cowhands who ride for the Big Ranch. You know, the one in the sky. Often when the sun shined on him, it really shined.

When the familiar shiny pickup and trailer of Dr. John's pulled into Pops' barnyard, it was obvious that something was up. Earlier in the year when Cooper had ridden the pair of black ponies for Dr. John, they had been left at their place for a couple of extra weeks while Coop had continued to ride and work with them.

"I came to settle up with you for the extra time you put on my ponies," Dr. John explained. "I can go ahead and pay you money or I have another idea that you just might like a little better. How would you like to have Banjo for your very own? I am offering him to you in trade for the time you put on my ponies earlier. What do you say?"

Cooper could not say "Yes!" fast enough.

"Then it's a deal," Dr. John said as he reached out his hand to shake Coop's. "I just happen to have him in the trailer, you know, just in case you said yes. Should we get him out?"

Cooper was already racing to the back of the trailer. "Hold on a minute, cowboy, aren't you gonna check with the boss before you agree to bring another pony around here?" Pops half-heartedly protested.

"You mean ask Mom?" he queried. "She won't mind, but I'll ask her if you think I ought to."

"That's not exactly what I had in mind," Pops started in to explain, then quickly realized it was futile to sort out the situation with this over-excited boy, so he just said, "Yeah, you're right. She won't mind at all." Banjo was there for keeps.

Because Banjo was worth much more than Cooper was owed, Coop agreed that he'd do some more riding for Dr. John down the line to make up the difference. After several years, the painted pony had returned. Banjo and Coop were together again.

Dandy was not easily replaced, but Banjo did his best to fill the big hole the Shetland pony had left. Coop could now drive a faster cart, jump bigger logs, race bigger horses, and ride with the best of the white hats on his very own "High Ho Silver" pony. Life was as good as it could be. Fall was in full swing, the cattle roundups had gone well, and snow was in the air. Banjo's hair started to grow into a long, thick winter coat, which accentuated his dark eyes and black hooves and made his stubby ears look even stubbier. He was all furry just like a little white polar bear.

For many winters, Pops had wintered the horses about two miles away from the house at the Lazy Two Ranch feedlot, along with their herd. This was a long-standing arrangement between Pops and the ranch and it had worked out very well. The ranch supplied the feed while the boys and Pops would wade through the snow daily to keep the herd fed and make sure the ice was broken off the water so the horses could drink.

It's important to understand what happens when herds are

merged together. All the horses have to find their place in the natural pecking order. The boss horse is determined and that dictates who eats first, who eats most, and who eats last. It's pretty much the same as what a bunch of school kids do when they are left on their own in the lunch line or school yard. This ritual takes a few weeks to get sorted out and typically leaves a few scars and bite marks on some rumps and sides as reminders of who should respect whom.

Even with feisty young horses, some sour old geldings, and several ornery broodmares in the herd, old Lily would always find her way to the top of the pecking order, year after year. Since Banjo was new to the herd, Lily tended to watch out for him, the same way she had watched out for Cooper all those years. Like Momma K always said, Lily was special.

Three nights before Christmas, the unthinkable happened. A gate at one end of the ten-acre pasture was left open and the horses got out. By studying the tracks later, it was easy to see that the herd had milled around for a while outside the fence, digging in the snow for tall dry grass before finding themselves on a side road in the pitch black of the cold winter night. One can only imagine the fright the horses had when suddenly out of the dark, glaring yellow headlights bore down on them like a speeding iron predator. As horses will, they spooked and started running. Their sharp hooves would have clattered as they bolted on the frozen pavement, a mass of ghostly fleeing figures shrouded in a mist of steam produced by their hot breath and excited bodies. Likely they were led by Lily, who ran—directed by instinct, fear, and a need for safety—toward Pops', the most familiar and secure place to her. In so doing, they had to cross a busy highway full of unsuspecting and fast-moving cars. In a thundering flash, they would have made a break for it, nearly flying across the roadway. It must have been like threading a one-inch rope through the eye of a needle, at high speed, no less! Miraculously, the entire racing herd made it through the traffic, as far as they knew.

The whole family was at the dinner table when the telephone rang. For some reason it seemed like an urgent ring. Momma K answered and her expression was one of genuine concern. She turned to the family with the story of the herd's escape, "They'd been seen stampeding this direction," she explained.

Immediately, the entire family rushed outside and found horses running all around the house. Then a flurry of additional phone calls came in from concerned neighbors, alerting them to what had happened. The older boys helped Pops corral the herd and settle

"Rush Hour"

them down, while Cooper kept asking, "Where is Banjo? Why can't I see him? What happened?" They were all there except for one.

With fearful hearts, they climbed in the truck and raced up to the busy highway. Once they got to the highway, they could see a crash site not far away. As they cautiously approached, the scene was unsettling, disturbing, and sad. There was a lingering smell of burnt brakes, hot bent metal, shattered glass, and heated horseflesh. Dust and frost still stirred and floated through the eerie glow of various angled and confused headlight beams and the relentless flashing red and blue lights of the officer's patrol truck.

Pops stopped and parked on the side of the road. They slowly got out and walked toward the center of all the commotion. It was surreal how the bustling bystanders, the concerned neighbors, and the investigating police officers whirled about them with a flurry of questions. It felt like life was in fast forward and slow motion all at the same time. Each movement seemed to last forever and accomplish nothing. Finally, they got to the heart of the scene and their worst fears were confirmed.

They felt so helpless beside Cooper. There was no way to protect him from the tragic sight, yet he insisted on being there. He was trying so hard to be helpful and strong, but right there before him laid his trusted friend, slowly growing colder on the frosty-hard, unfeeling ground at the side of the road. Pops forced himself into motion, hurrying to get a flatbed trailer and calling a friend to bring a backhoe. When the equipment was all there, Banjo was lifted up onto the trailer as carefully as possible. As they raised the pony's body, Cooper pleaded to Pops and the men who were helping, uttering a string of heartbreaking concerns through a tear-choked voice.

"Be careful. Don't hurt him. Please be nice to him. Don't make him bleed!" he muttered through quivering lips. His little heart was breaking. Cooper clung to his mother as tightly as he could with his trembling little hands. His whole body shook as tears flowed down his flushed, damp cheeks. The boy's mind was surely flooded with memories and more pain than a little feller should ever have to endure. Even though Banjo had no more cares in this world, Coop could not cease to cry over him. Most everyone couldn't help but cry with him. It turned out to be a long, dark night.

The herd they all got loose
A stampede through the snow in the dark
A running white little caboose
Tried to keep up with all of his heart.

The drivers in the night could not see
Where the frightened pony might be.
But in the end, the glow of the moon did show
A crimson stain, spilled on the pure white snow.

Early the next morning, Pops buried Banjo in the frozen ground next to the round pen in the barnyard, where his body could stay and be close to Coop forever. They believed that Banjo had gone quickly to a much better place. Pops comforted Cooper by saying, "You know he went to the Big Ranch, you know the one that we talk about, the one in the sky. Where the grass is always stirrup high, where he'll never be cold again. He'll never have to compete for feed, or be painted pink either," he consoled.

Banjo would surely be missed and the whole family was hurting

with and for Cooper. He now had a painful, lonely, empty space in his wounded little heart.

The tragedy was two days before Christmas. Normally such a happy time for youngsters, but for Cooper, this one was filled with tears and gloom. Banjo was gone, and Dandy, though still close by, was not really his anymore. He felt alone without a pony, a friend. That oh-so-sweet connection had been unfairly broken. Of course, if Coop had not known such high pony times, he would not have now felt so low.

Cooper was not sure if he even wanted Christmas to come, but it came anyway. When the blessed morning arrived, he didn't even attempt to crawl out of bed. He thought of Olivia, how she would be hugging her new pony, Flashlight. He was happy for her, but it was also a hurtful, stinging reminder of his loss.

"Cooper, it's time to get up. Come and see if Santa came," Momma K and the kids coaxed. Before the Banjo tragedy, Pops and Momma K had helped Santa Claus pick out some really nice buckaroo spurs for Cooper. They were

silver mounted with fancy tooled straps, jingle bobs, and big shiny rowels. They had been so sure that these would be the perfect gift, but Coop wasn't taking pleasure in anything for now.

Pops took a different approach. He said, "Coop, get up and before you look at any presents, you need to go collect eggs and feed Kristie's horses." The whole family cast looks of astonishment at each other and wondered. How could he be so insensitive?

Fortunately, Cooper was numb to it all. Since he was not feeling particularly festive, he might as well be doing his regular chores. He went outside, away from the others and the noise and celebrating that went along with what was supposed to be a merry event. Coop bundled up and trudged to the barnyard. From the way he was moving, it appeared that he was in no hurry to get there and likely in no hurry to get back.

For what seemed like forever, Pops could not help but hover at the back door. It was likely that the kids and their mother were all thinking to themselves, "He sure is heartless sending Coop out on Christmas morning to do chores and then spying on him to make sure he gets them done." Well Pops had his ways and that was that.

All of a sudden, Cooper came running from the barnyard,

pounding on the back door and hollering with excitement.

"Come see! Come see what I got!"

Startled, the family came busting out of the house. They were falling all over each other in their hurry to see what he was so fired up about.

He had a pony by the halter rope and not just any pony. It was Blue Eclipse and the pony had a big red bow tied around his neck.

"He's for me," Coop exclaimed, so sure of himself.

"How do you figure that the pony is for you?" Pops asked, hiding a smile.

"He just has to be. He was down in a stall with this big red ribbon tied around his neck. He just has to be for me!" Cooper was beaming and bubbling with excitement. The Christmas spirit had finally arrived in full force and it was showing all over the little cowboy's beaming face.

"Do you feel like seein' your other Christmas presents now?" Annie asked. She was so anxious for him to see what she had gotten for him.

What a turn around, a happy day after all! The Christmas angels were definitely singing a heavenly tune. Was that Banjo accompaniment?

All thanks to the Cowboss at the Big Ranch.

"Black Tornado"

Coop was as proud as a little Banty Rooster

15. JOHNNY

After all the morning festivities and surprises had settled down and there was some quiet time, Momma K cornered Pops and said, "How did you? And when did you get that pony in a stall down at the barnyard? I know Santa Claus and I don't think he's that magic."

"I don't know what you're talkin' about. I know Santa too and he must be magic because I didn't have anything to do with it," Pops could not be trusted in times like this and he was getting the most out of this one.

"How did you pay for that pony? I know that he was priced up there pretty high," Momma K said, sounding concerned.

"You'll know soon enough how it all came together and I think you'll be very impressed and surprised." Pops was being more tight-lipped than ever and she could not figure out how he had pulled this off. He just let her stew on it for a time before he finally spilled the beans.

She just needed to know!

Unknown to most of the family, someone else had learned about the events on the highway. They also knew of Blue Eclipse and the work Cooper had done with him. Like Pops said, news in a small town travels fast. Without hesitation, that person contacted Mrs.

Yeager and offered to purchase the pony. After they had filled Mrs. Yeager in on the entire situation, she came down on the price to help in making the big surprise happen. Then, late on Christmas Eve, by themselves, they quietly snuck the pony into one of the stalls in Pops' barnyard. Then Santa, alias Dr. John, tied the big red bow on the pony's neck and left it there for Cooper to find Christmas morning.

Obviously the vast ranges and pastures of the Big Ranch aren't too wide for the cowboys who ride there to cross. It's important to remember that those angels riding herd for the little ones down here can help make some very special things happen.

Once they all discovered who the "Pony Angel" was, Cooper made an announcement. "I'm changing the pony's name. I like Blue, but I'm going to name him 'Johnny Blue' and I'll call him 'Johnny' for short."

Momma K called Dr. John to hug him through the phone, thank him, and wish him a happy Christmas. He simply said, "Well, I have always had a soft spot in my heart for kids and ponies. I guess I feel like they should just be together. That's all." She filled him in on the pony's new name and he said he liked that.

Momma K's eyes were tearing up that entire day. In fact, there was not a dry eye in the whole house. It is said that a privileged cowboy is lucky to have one real good horse, one dog of equal caliber, and maybe know a few truly good people in his lifetime. But Cooper, in his short cowboy life, had already well surpassed those marks. If the adage was true, he had the blessing of knowing way more than his share.

It had lightly snowed during the night, gently covering the dark soil of Banjo's fresh grave. Being covered with a soft white blanket,

"Cold Shadows"

the barnyard was reminiscent of a blank painter's canvas. The morning sun was shining brightly on a new day as Pops thought to himself, This will be a Christmas to remember.

Though Pops had not been the giver of the Christmas pony, the experience became a solid link in the pony connection between him and Coop. Their work was cut out for them because Johnny Blue was a lot of pony. He needed many hours of gentle handling and sweaty saddle blankets for him to become a real cowpony—to measure up to Dandy and Banjo.

To further train Johnny and to help Cooper gain more confidence, they repeated the same careful process that they had used when the pony came the first time, a refresher course one might say. First, they got Johnny accustomed to wearing a harness and a bridle. Then, they taught him to drive by putting him in the round pen and walking behind him while steering him with a very long pair of reins. Coop would turn the pony right and left, stop him, back him up, then go forward, speed up, slow down, then do it all again over and over. Those two went around and around the pen until Johnny had relaxed and was accepting whatever was asked of him.

After a few days, they added a saddle and drove him some more. It was not long before Cooper was riding his pony, working him  hard all spring and into the summer. Johnny was plenty fiery and only three years old. By midsummer, the pony had many miles on him and was pretty much ready for anything Cooper could cook up.

Pops recalls the day Cooper's respect for Johnny's fire was taken to an extreme. They were considering how well Johnny's driving training had gone and Coop asked, "Why don't we see how he will do with the cart?"

With wise caution, Pops decided to first hitch that pony to a training sled that was heavy and had more resistance to keep Johnny from running away with it. They again started in the round pen, a fairly controlled environment. That went well, so they took him out into the pasture, a less controlled environment. A couple of successful times around the pasture and Coop was soon his old over-confident self, so much that he relaxed and lay flat on his back in the training sled, gazing up at the lazily drifting clouds and blue summer sky.

To this day, Pops is not completely sure what happened next. It was all kind of a blur. All he can figure is Johnny spooked and in the blink of a terrified eye and about three jumps, Coop's pony was up to full speed. Like a shot out of a gun, he was on a dead run and looking for an opening to get out of the pasture. Cooper sat straight up in the sled, eyes wide and looking for his own way out of the situation. He had lost both of the reins and they were headed straight for a five-foot high cross-buck fence. Johnny was running flat out and full throttle. He had the sled that was supposedly too heavy to go too fast, especially with Cooper in it, generally airborne. About every thirty feet, the sled touched down with a neck-breaking jolt, and then it would awkwardly set sail again. It was Cooper and the sled behind a runaway pony, but it looked more like a whipping and snapping banner on a stressed flagpole in the middle of a hurricane.

When they were about 100 feet from the fence, Coop came to his senses. "Mom," he said later, "I knew Johnny was going over that fence come rain or shine. I thought on my choices, which were few. Mom, I knew how to fall out, and I was scared of hitting that fence, so I bailed."

Watching from a distance, Pops was uncertain what was going to happen next. Could Johnny jump a five-foot fence with a heavy sled in tow? The pony did not break stride or even hesitate. With neck stretched out straight, head cocked, nostrils flared, and hooves flying, he sailed right over the buck rail fence. He cleared the fence easily, but the sled crashed right through all four of the five-inch rails. Johnny and the sled burst out the other side like a high school football team smashing through a banner at a homecoming game.

Having landed in Kristie's pasture, Johnny raced in huge circles until the harness broke and the sled went tumbling into the far fence. Then he slowed down and settled back on earth. His eyes were bulging and intense. His sides were heaving in and out as he struggled to catch his breath through wide-stretched nostrils. He was lathered in sweat that ran off his shoulders and hind legs, pooling on the dusty ground.

Pops ran to help however he could. He discovered that both Coop and Johnny had some bumps and scratches, which to a young cowboy and his cowpony, are badges of honor and evidence of a great adventure. The wreck had made a big mess. A section of the fence was shattered, the sled was beat up, and the harness was broken, but those things could be repaired. Pops was very grateful that neither Coop nor Johnny was seriously injured, a genuine miracle!

Coop's own fire now flamed high. He was fighting mad at what his pony had done. He said to Johnny, "What do you think you are doing running off like that? You could have killed both of us!" He liberally sprinkled in a few barnyard words to more fully express his frustration. His mother was shocked, and no doubt wondered where he had learned such language. Pops could not imagine, for the life of him, where Coop could have learned to talk like that.

Pops stopped Coop in his rant and said, "If you would have been sittin' up tall the whole time, this wouldn't have happened."

Cowboy philosophy says if you can't get to the bottom of why two cats don't get along, just tie their tails together and let them fight it out. Although Johnny needed to learn how to be a better-behaved pony, it was evident that Cooper had some behavior learning to do, as well. Pops retrieved the pony, removed what was left of the harness, and put a saddle on him. To say the least, Cooper was shook up and did not want any part of this. "I'm not getting on him right now," he protested.

Pops knew it was best for Cooper to get on Johnny and ride him. He subscribed to the old thinking, "When you get thrown off, the best thing to do is get right back on." With some encouragement and reassurance that he would be okay, the young cowboy crawled

"Strong Willed"

on. It was a little shaky at first, but he and Johnny were soon riding off to rebuild the trust between them.

With the fences now mended, including the cross buck one, the growing experience behind them, a few more sweaty saddle blankets, and many more miles down the road, Cooper and Johnny were again starting to share the same shadow, to think as one, and continuing to build a very special and unique connection.

One day while moving cattle through the hills, Coop and Johnny covered about 1,800 acres before they made their way home. They'd traveled all sorts of terrain, deep washes, and thick stands of oak brush and sagebrush flats. Upon returning, Cooper realized that the rowel along with the jingle bobs from one of his Christmas spurs was missing. With all of the distance covered that day, it would be impossible to find them. He felt terrible because the rowel was custom made and would be nearly impossible to match, yet the thought of "finding a needle in a hay stack" looked easy compared to finding the rowel on the range. He always hoped it would show up, but in the meantime, with Pop's help, he went ahead and got new matching rowels and jingle-bobs. Cooper kept the original misfit rowel on a shelf as a keepsake from a very special Christmas, and as a reminder to never, ever give up.

"Priceless"
You can't place a dollar amount
on the value of a Quarter Horse

"Quarter Horse"

16. IRON PONY ADVENTURES

Pops and Momma K were forever trying to come up with a business plan that would allow them to expand the family income potential, stay in the horse world, and share this cowboy lifestyle and experience with others. After throwing some ideas around and doing some research, they put together a scheme. It was an outfit called "Iron Pony Adventures." Tourists and people from the city would surely want to experience the things that the family did on an everyday basis. Pops was sure of it.

He took it up with the kids. "What do you think of this idea of catering to the public?" he asked them. The consensus was "Let's go for it!" Besides, this adventure was sure to spawn many tales to be retold down the road.

They started by contracting with the Garden of Eden horse farm to use their scenic and accessible ranch to offer trail rides. Then they hung out their shingle. The daily duties were divided up. Levi, Isaac, and Coop were to help feed, water, and care for the trail horses each day. They were also responsible for helping catch and saddle the horses. Cheyenne was to answer phones and help keep them all organized. It was a good fit. At twelve years old, Coop was the youngest wrangler.

In addition to those duties, Cooper and the boys soon found

themselves guiding groups of tourists on trail rides. Leaving from the barnyard with anywhere from two to twelve riders in tow, they

would head out across the meadows, travel down through the big shady cottonwood trees of the bottoms, and up the Middle Fork River. The boys would point out deer and other wildlife along the way, then they'd circle back to the barn.

Cooper liked to jabber and see people have fun. "Hey look there, did you see that big buck runnin' through the brush?" or "Look way up there in that big cottonwood tree. That's a bald eagle, neat huh?" were just a few of the observations he would point out to the groups. Sometimes he'd even spot a bear or a lion or even an elephant, but all of those critters mysteriously vanished into the woods before the tourists could get a glimpse of them. "Oh you just missed it," he'd say. Plenty of "Big Foot" stories were also tossed around. It was all in fun and by the time the ride was over, those he was guiding were sure enough comfortable and they felt like old friends.

"Hey, Coop, what's that jinglin' in your pocket?" Pops asked.

"Oh nothin," Coop nonchalantly responded.

Overhearing Pops' question, Isaac complained, "Did he get money again?"

"Again? Tell me about this, Coop."

"He's always gettin' money from the tourists. They seem to like his babbling, so at the end of lots of the rides people just give him money," Isaac again spoke up.

"Maybe you should talk up yourself and you'd get the same," Levi suggested.

"What do you mean?" Isaac was now all ears.

Levi tipped his hat up and spoke big, "We got a deal worked out, me and Coop. I guide the people, he jabbers through the whole ride and keeps 'em laughin', then at the end of the ride he gets the tips and we split up the money."

"I want in!" Isaac chimed.

Over time the boys ended up being rewarded handsomely with tips.

After a couple fun-packed seasons had passed and winter was coming on again, Pops moved the operation to another place in the valley where they offered bobsleigh rides to that same sort of customers. The horse-drawn bobsleigh that they used was an old time one that had been used to feed livestock in the wintertime. The classic wooden runners of the old bobs were painted yellow and adorned with black pinstripes. The runners were wrapped with hand-forged iron designed for carrying heavy loads and they had done their job faithfully for many, many years. For breaking through deep, wind-crusted snow or sliding freely on a packed trail, there was nothing better or more traditional than an old set of bobs.

Pops had the old sleigh around for a long time and it wasn't so romantic to the kids. "We're gonna use that old thing?" They questioned.

"Yeah, people will like it," Pops said. "It'll be all new to 'em. You'll see."

Pops' claims turned out to be true. The sleigh box would creak and moan while twisting over the terrain, expressing its age and sharing its stories with the guests and caroling families. It proved to be every bit as romantic as riding in a classic two-horse open sleigh if you threw in a cozy patchwork quilt and some hot chocolate.

The Wild Bunch loved their team, an enormous pair of Shire draft horses, and those horses could pull. There was Butch, a huge horse with hindquarters deserving of a "Wide Load" sign. He had a massive arching neck and the surprising energy of a puppy. Because of his look, they often referred to him as a monster pony. Then there was his harness mate, Macey. She was the anchor, slightly smaller and older, a willing constant, making the team steady and efficient.

Coop and Isaac both helped take care of the horses, including feeding, watering, and blanketing them each night to keep them warm. Most nights, the pair of them would come home tired and half frozen to the bone from many hours of driving the horses in cold weather. Pops was so proud of them for their dedication and work ethic. Besides harnessing and driving, Cooper and Isaac helped load the guests on the sleigh, making sure they were comfortable. Just like he had done on the trail rides, Cooper would visit with the patrons. He'd tell stories and talk about the horses as they drove, his young voice accompanied by the sound of the jingling sleigh bells. Part of what made the hard, cold work doable was the opportunity for interaction with other folks. Coop and Isaac were doing all this at the ages of fourteen and seventeen.

The sleigh rides took place in a large snowy meadow near Wolf Mountain. After many trips around the meadow hauling happy customers, a good trail had formed and was frozen hard. This helped to make for a smooth ride and also made it fairly easy for the horses to travel.

That first winter that Cooper drove the team, the snow became extremely deep. It just kept piling up. One evening between Christmas and New Year's, a big storm out of the north came over

The teamsters

the mountains and into the valley. Pops was helping the boys on that particular night. They watched as it curled over the tops of the Rocky Mountains and down the craggy cliffs like some kind of abominable, bluish-gray monster, clawing its way over the terrain. The storm smothered the valley and the wind started to blow. It turned into a blizzard like none of them had ever seen before or since. Thunder and lightning even cracked, boomed, and shot across the sky, which is very rare during a snow storm. It was scary in its strangeness.

They were in the middle of a ride when that storm came raging over the mountaintops. The family on the ride had small children. The crew was concerned that the children were not dressed especially warm. The father asked, "Can we go back to the barn now?"

"You bet. Anything you want," Pops was happy to oblige them. They trotted the horses quickly back to the barn. It was such a whiteout that he could not see, so he ducked his head and trusted that the horses knew the way. Once at the barn, they skipped having hot chocolate with the guests and hustled to get the horses unhitched and put up for the night. They hopped in the truck and raced for home.

By the next morning, all the fences and bushes, along with anything else less than six feet tall, were totally consumed in a sea of white. It was nearly impossible to tell where the original sleigh trail had been. The fields looked like oceans with enormous frozen banks resembling curling waves. Visibility was next to nothing. The storm continued blowing clouds of snow. Rides were scheduled for that day, but Pops said, "We better see if we can find the trail before we attempt to take guests out there."

"I'll go do it," Cooper offered.

"I think I better go with you just in case something happens." They bundled up and trudged toward the snow-covered horses.

First, they shoveled away a mountain of snow that covered the sleigh, then dug down to expose its runners. They pulled the blankets off the team (Pops was sure that Butch and Macey weren't happy about that) and Coop helped harness and hitch them to the sleigh. When the horses first attempted to go forward, the sleigh did not budge.

"This thing is frozen down solid," Pops said to Cooper. They shoveled more snow away from the runners and Pops chipped at the ice that had built up around them. By using the team to pivot the tongue of the sleigh back and forth, the runners soon worked loose. The old sleigh twisted and moaned under the strain of the extreme horsepower, but once free to move, the team cautiously headed out in search of the trail.

As they traveled, a large pile of snow quickly built up in front of the sleigh. The horses had to work hard as they struggled for good footing while pulling the extra weight of the accumulating snow. As long as they stayed on the original trail, they were able to keep moving. There were a few recognizable landmarks still visible above the snow, like some tall trees and posts which helped to guide Pops for the most part. Part way round the meadow, the trail came up over what was previously a small rise but was now piled high with a tremendous amount of snow. The constant blowing made it difficult to see and pretty much impossible to tell where the trail was.

"Can you see anything?" Pops asked Coop.

"Not really. Can you? Just let the horses have their heads and they'll pick their way along," he was confident. They hunched over, protecting themselves from the pelting storm. Driving blind, they put their trust in the horses, hoping they could find the way. They carefully eased along. Once the sleigh crested the rise and started down the other side, the horses lost their way and stumbled blindly off the trail. In the deep, untracked snow, the sleigh and the team all but disappeared. The huge horses dropped like rocks in water, sinking in snow up to the top of their backs. They lunged forward and tried to swim out of the relentless sea of white, but the sleigh was too heavy and bogged in. The horses were getting tired and could not get sure footing. The powdery snow was too much for them. All the horsepower in the world doesn't do any good if it can't get any traction.

"I'm sure glad we didn't have any riders on board!" Pops thought out loud.

"Yeah, me too. I bet that would have given them a big scare," Coop agreed.

Pops carefully got off the sleigh. "Hold the lines," he told Cooper. "Stay on the sleigh and be ready to drive. If nothing else, just hang onto the horses." He made his way down alongside the horses. He sunk waist deep and moving was a struggle. Nevertheless, he managed to dig down alongside the horses to where the harness tugs connected to the double tree on the sleigh. He went to work undoing the harness and unhitching the team.

Being down in the snow with the horses was difficult and dangerous. "Coop, this is a risky deal, you need to hang on to those lines and be ready for whatever happens," he cautioned. Cooper had his work cut out for him holding the lines and making sure the team stayed put until it was time for them to move forward. While those two shires would never have intended to hurt anyone, in the course of their struggling they could easily crush a person with their massive bodies or their floundering hooves. Pops finally got the team unhitched and then waded out of the way and encouraged Butch and Macey to swim out. At first, they looked at Pops and started to move his way.

"Coop! Keep their heads straight!" he hollered. "Don't let them climb on top of me!" Cooper hung on to the lines, straightened them out, hopped off of the sleigh, and swam along behind them. He did a great job keeping the horses controlled. Once the horses thrashed their way back up to the security of the solid trail, they were exhausted. They left the sleigh and trailed the horses back to the barn where they fed and re-blanketed them.

"The horses have had it," Pops said and Cooper agreed. "I think we're a little used up, too. What do you say we come back later and figure out how to get that sleigh unstuck? I hope we don't have to leave it until spring before we can get at it." The sleigh rides had to be cancelled for the day.

The next day, under better weather conditions, Cooper, Isaac, and Pops went back to get the sleigh unstuck. They harnessed both horses and led them out to the stranded sleigh. With renewed horsepower, and a little redneck engineering, they had a plan to get the job done.

"Here, hold the horses, Coop," Pops muttered as he was concentrating.

"What do you plan to do?" Coop asked. Did Pops have a plan? These things are dealt with as they come, this life is a constant test of

creativity. How can you really have a plan?

"I think I'll pull the tongue around toward the trail and kind of jack-knife it. Then we can string that log chain through the end of the tongue and tie Butch's harness tugs together and hook the chain in the end of them. That ought to do it," Pops said.

"What do you want me to do now?" Coop asked.

"You'd better take Macey back out of the way because there's not much footing here and Butch is going to need all he can get."

"Do you think he can do it all by himself?" Isaac asked.

"I'm afraid he'll have to. There just isn't enough room for both horses on this trail at once."

Pops cautiously led Butch forward as Macey stood by watching. "Step up, Butch," he encouraged. The big horse showed his power and heart as he bore down. With one big heave, he pulled that sleigh right up out of the deep snow trench and back onto the trail.

"Wow that was impressive!" Coop cheered. "That's some horsepower! He's tough, isn't he Pops?"

"He sure is," Pops said with pride. "I guess we now know what our plan was," Pops added.

Once the sleigh was back on the firm trail, they checked it over. Fortunately, it was unharmed, so they hitched up the team and went on to give many more rides for the rest of the season, though much less eventful ones. Pops was glad of that.

When spring came, there were plenty more Iron Pony stories to tell. The family sat down to talk and came to the conclusion that they'd had enough fun in this adventure. Pops said, "What do you all think of ending this business venture and trying a new one?"

They all agreed saying, "Let's go for it!"

"Partners"

"Chief Brown Horse"

17. GROWIN' UP AND MOVIN' ON

Levi missed out on the bobsleigh fun that winter. He had graduated high school by then and was smart enough to hire on with some old friends of Pops' who lived in Arizona (a good place to spend the winter, especially that winter).

These friends owned a trail riding business and were very successful. Sometimes they would take as many as 300 people a day on horse rides through the desert. Levi was out riding around in his shirt-sleeves while the boys at home were swimming around in record-deep snow. Not hard to see who the smart one was. He was there for just a few months, but he chose the right months.

When Levi came home in the spring, he approached Pops. "Hey Dad, what would you think of me looking for a job on a ranch somewhere other than around here?"

Pops could tell that he'd been considering this for a while now, and having been out of the nest for a time, his independence was taking over. It's one of those things a parent looks forward to and dreads at the same time, but the fledglings have got to try their own wings sometime.

"What do you have in mind?" Pops asked.

"I don't exactly know," Levi said thoughtfully. "But someplace big and in some country that I've never seen before, with all new cattle and people. I guess something totally different, you know, greener pastures or maybe some place where I can find my destiny?"

"Boy you have been thinking about this," Pops mumbled. "And who is Destiny?" he teased.

With temporary frustration, Levi said, "Dad, you know what I mean!"

Pops thought, that sounds exciting to me. "How can I help you?" he offered.

"Do you know anyone who runs a place like I'm talking about that we could call and see about a job?" He sure was sincere about this idea.

"I'll think on it and see what I can come up with," Pops responded.

Pops got on the phone and talked to some rancher friends from around the country to see what was out there for a young feller. He wasn't searching for anything permanent, Pops didn't believe, just a seasonal cowboy job to try his luck and gain some experience. It just so happened that a friend of a friend had the perfect situation for Levi, a cowboy job on a huge place called the Padlock Ranch near Sheridan, Wyoming. By the end of April, he was hired. In this new country, he gained some experience alright. He got more saddle time, roped more calves, and doctored more range cattle than he had ever seen before. He loved the country and the cow boss, Jesse.

While he was on the Padlock, a regional leatherwork show was held in Sheridan. Levi had always had an interest in working with leather, so on one of his days off he drove in to town to check out the show. As he was browsing through the vendors and displays, he ran into a man he hadn't seen for nearly eighteen years. His name was Kent.

Kent did not recognize him because Levi was just a little boy the last time they met. Twenty years before, Kent was a next door neighbor but had since moved to Idaho where he had perfected the art of saddle making. Through a lot of hard work and talent, he had

"Watering on the Padlock"

become one of the best and most well-known buckaroo style saddle makers in the country.

Levi and Kent had a great visit and as they were parting, Kent asked the usual questions, "How's your family and the old home town and all of the neighbors, etc.?" But the best thing he asked Levi was, "What are you up to nowadays?"

"I'm riding for the Padlock, you know, just cowboyin' for the season. I also do a little leather work on the side. I just make gear to use myself like bridles and belts. I did make a purse for a girl I know and it turned out okay. She kept it."

"Well, when are you done at the Padlock?" Kent probed.

"In a couple of months I should be finished up," Levi said.

"Then what are you going to do?"

"I guess I'll head back home and look for work around there."

"Why don't you come to work for me? We'll see if we can turn you into a saddle maker."

Destiny?

"Dakota"

When Levi was done on the ranch, he came home for a week or so, then Pops helped move him to Idaho. Once he was there, he was thrown headlong into an apprenticeship of saddle making. The learning curve was very steep, but he was excited and up for the challenge. What an opportunity.

The shop he went to work for, Frecker Saddlery, specialized in custom buckaroo saddles for a select clientele from around the world. The saddles were built from the ground up. They first carve out a wooden shape called a tree and then cover it with rawhide. Next is the tanned leather and so on, to the finished, beautifully tooled, silver-clad product. The saddles are extremely functional as well as impressive showpieces.

A call Pops received a short time later from Levi went something like, "Guess what I did, Dad!"

"I'm not too good at guessing, so you're going to have to tell me what you did."

"Well, you know that saddle that I bought a while before I went to work at the Padlock?"

"Yeah, I remember you were kind of proud of it," Pops reminded him.

"I got it good and broke in and changed out the stirrups for better ones, and I put on a new horn wrap, too, so it was working and looking pretty good. Well, I put it up for sale for more than I bought it for, and it sold!"

"Good for you. Now what's your plan?" Pops wondered out loud.

"You remember ever since I fell off that saddle in Kemmerer when we were stayin' in that old sheep camp back when me and Isaac were kids? I said then I was going to have one someday that was built just for me, you know, one that would fit me just right? Well Kent has custom built me a tree and I am about half done buildin' it. Yeah, I'm pretty excited to try it out!" He could hardly contain himself. "I think I'm going to make it what's called a Hamley Daisy pattern."

"I am excited for you and I can hardly wait to see when you get it done. Keep me up to date on how it's comin' along," Pops added.

"I should have it all done soon, and I'll send you a picture for sure."

"That's great. Good for you." Many a good cowboy rides tall in the saddle, but very few can do so in a saddle they've built themselves, one that fits just right.

Levi's Hamley Daisy

"Equally Yoked"

18. A HANG'N CRIME

Coop and his brothers (when they were around) continued to help with riding and training horses. Annie was consumed with her studies, her clothes, and her friends. Momma K kept the place running. And Pops kept painting.

"Hey! Troy called again," Coop said as he came running out to where Pops was working.

"Oh, what did he have to say?"

"He said they are comin' here from Arizona to be in the Pioneer Days parade next month. I guess some feed and ranch supply store is sponsoring them to bring their eight-horse hitch to be in the parade and advertise their store," Cooper reported. "Then a few weeks after that, they are takin' the same hitch of horses to compete at the county fair."

"Does he want some help while they're here? Did he say anything about needin' a place for the horses to stay between the events?" Pops wondered as he kept on working.

"I think so. He said he

would call later and talk to you when you're not busy, then you can ask him all of that stuff yourself." Then Coop was on his way.

From time to time, Pops boarded Troy's draft horses as he was traveling through the area. An eight-horse hitch is a showstopper and promotes a sponsoring business well. The flashiest show teams are evenly matched in every aspect. They try to match for size, color, markings, and gait. The horses in this hitch were black with white stocking legs and white strips down their faces. The first two horses nearest the wagon (called the "wheel" horses) tend to be the biggest, most powerful pullers. This was the job for Tess and Bev, two massive and very experienced mares. The next two sets of horses must also be seasoned and patient, willing to stay calm and work between other horses, regardless of what their teammates may be up to. These teams were made up of Quade and Zeb followed by Kit and Doll. The lead team is not so much for pulling power. They may be the most important part of the rig for keeping everything in control, so they must be great leaders. This was the job for Talley and Poppy, two perfectly matched, flashy mares who had been

HORSE

pulling together since they were young. Obviously, it takes years to put a team like this together.

Prior to the event, the team was hitched many times and several maneuvers were practiced to ensure success on the parade route, which would be lined with thousands of noisy spectators. Before the celebration, the horses were meticulously bathed, their manes and tails braided and laced with ribbons. The harnesses were polished and shined up, and the wagon decorated with sponsor banners. It was because of this impressive team that Troy was asked to participate in the big parade.

Troy said, "I think we're ready."

A parade manager hollered, "Get ready to line up. You're next."

Pops turned and asked, "Okay, Troy, where do you want me?"

"Once we're all hitched, I need you ridin' shotgun up here on the seat by me. Your job will be to take the lines for short spells when I get tired and to wave at the crowds, you know, act like you're having fun. We've gotta put on a little bit of a show for the people."

"Sounds good to me," Pops said as he scrambled up on the seat.

Troy went on to instruct the rest of the help, "Now I need all you guys to out ride on both sides of the team. Spread out and just be ready to help if a harness comes undone or something breaks or some little kids or a dog runs out onto the road. You just got to watch out for anything that might turn into a problem."

Troy commanded, "Tally! Poppy! Step up, come on girls, step up, it's time to go!" At that simple command, an intense chain reaction of horsepower was set into motion, starting with the lead team and rippling back until the wagon lurched forward and they were moving. Once moving, it was an incredible sight to see. The Budweiser horses in the Super Bowl ads have nothing over on this rig! The team performed the six mile parade route flawlessly. The crowds of thousands waved and cheered as the team majestically eased by them. A string of one-ton horses, lined up two by two, four horses deep, traveling down the road, driven by a single teamster is impressive and nearly impossible to appreciate unless you have been right in the middle of it.

After the parade, the horses were brought back to rest in a pasture near Pops' house. The location was perfect for their recuperation, 50 acres of leftover alfalfa hay field, a meadow, and a reservoir fed

"Grey Train"

by a little meandering stream. It was secluded in a valley out of sight and away from the noise of traffic. When they first turned them out, those big horses ran and bucked like a bunch of young foals playing for the first time. They soon settled in to grazing in the meadow and lounging in the shade of the trees.

As they turned them loose, Troy watched and commented, "Well they ought to be happy and safe here for a few weeks."

Bob, the pasture manager, asked, "How long do you need to leave them here?"

"They're not scheduled for another job for about a month, so I guess I'll come get them just before that. I'll call you ahead of time." Troy then left to go back to Arizona. Before he headed out, he asked Cooper to keep track of the horses.

For the first week that the horses were in the pasture it was beautiful weather. Then as it can do in the high mountains, it turned bad and there were a couple of drenching thunderstorms. They lit up the night sky and soaked the area. After one storm, Cooper rode a horse over to check on the team again. He soon came racing home in an obvious panic.

"What's happening? What's wrong?" Pops asked.

Coop and the horse were struggling to catch their breath as he tried to answer Pop's questions. "I went to check on Troy's horses and I could only count seven. I couldn't see Poppy anywhere!"

"Where all did you look?" Pops pressed.

"I looked everywhere in the pasture and around the pond. I checked all the fences and gates, and she's not anywhere."

"Let's go look again," Pops said as they saddled fresh horses and headed back to the pasture. All the while, Pops was thinking the horse had to be there somewhere. Maybe she was just lying down in the tall grass or in the thick brush or just standing in the shade of the big trees. After an in-depth search, however, they came up empty-handed. By then Pops was really getting concerned. As he scanned the pasture he thought to himself, this doesn't look good.

Pops called out the search parties. On horseback, they searched the hills and neighboring pastures several more times. They looked up and down the creek bed. They even put on hip waders and walked all through the creek. They went so far as to drain the 3-acre, 20-foot-deep reservoir just in case the mare had slipped, lost her footing, and possibly drowned in it. They were all very glad to not find her in the pond, but it left the mystery unsolved. They checked and rechecked the fences.

"There's no way that big horse could have jumped any of these fences," Pops said many times. "These fences are in great shape, tight as piano string. Besides, if she had somehow gotten out of the pasture, she would have hung around rather than go wondering off. She wouldn't be willing to leave her herd, especially Tally."

"It just doesn't add up," was the consensus. After three days, it was starting to look very suspicious. With a horse so big, with black and white markings, grazing in a green pasture surrounded by easy terrain, finding her should be simple.

"Bob, do you have any ideas?" Pops was at the end of his rope, so to speak.

"As I go over and over it in my head, all I can come up with is it had to be someone who knows the area and the fence system. The only unlocked gates are hard to find so if she were taken out of a gate, it would have to have been by someone who knew their way around. Especially as hard as it was to see during that crazy storm and being as dark as it was," Bob deduced. "And it had to be

"Inseparable"

during the storm because we can't find any kind of tracks anywhere. I figure all signs were washed away by all the rain," he added.

"So do you think it was someone who works for you?" Pops cautiously inquired.

"Well I hate to think like that, but it sure looks that way. At least, it's someone who knows someone who works here. We'll keep an ear to the ground just in case."

Pops was also in regular contact with Troy who was literally pacing the floor in Arizona. He felt so helpless. In many states, horse stealing is still an offense punishable by hanging. Of course the punishment is never enforced, but when you have experienced what it's like when a horse has been stolen from you, well then it's easy to think, maybe it should still be an enforced punishment.

From the beginning, Pops had notified the police and other authorities. He'd contacted the local news agencies and put ads in all the newspapers. They visited every sale barn and auction yard, and contacted all the area veterinarians. Local and regional brand inspectors were put on alert, then in turn they put out the call for the big mare's return, but there were very few leads. They took it to the ground, spreading out and searching all the barns, sheds, big buildings, and the surrounding countryside for her. They chased every rumor and explored every possibility and prayed for help. At one point, they even enlisted the help of a psychic.

They continued to hunt for her.

On the third or fourth day that Poppy had been missing, the group was searching through an 1,800-acre pasture nearby. As Pops was riding up a deep dry wash, he noticed something shiny, but half covered with dirt on the ground. He got off to check it out.

"Well I'll be," Pops mumbled to himself. To his amazement, it was Cooper's missing spur rowel—the one that he had lost a long time before. They figured that thing was lost forever. Instantly, finding the rowel sparked renewed hope. What are the chances? Pops thought. If I could find such a relatively tiny thing in such a large area, surely there's a way to find that big horse after all.

They looked for Poppy for the better part of two weeks. No doubt about it, they were getting tired and discouraged. They had traveled the local area many times, and by now had even covered parts of three other states, as well. They had exhausted every idea that they could think of, with no luck finding her.

Troy came back from Arizona because it was time for the full team to go to their next event, the Eastern Idaho State Fair. He helped them hunt for a couple of days before they had to go. Without

Poppy, he was forced to reduce the team to a six-horse hitch. It was a heavy feeling when he pulled out of the yard that day.

When he got to Idaho, the news had preceded him. On the first night there, a man approached him and said, "I hear you had a horse come up missing. Do you think maybe someone stole it?" he questioned. He went on, "I have a friend who knows that area well and his family knows a lot of people there. I fly a helicopter and I'd be obliged to get my buddy and scour the place and see what we could stir up."

"I sure would appreciate that. We don't really know where else to look," Troy said.

Pops and the boys kept up the pressure and hunted on. Two days later, early in the morning, Pops got a call from Bob. "You've gotta come see this," he said with noticeable relief in his voice.

Pops didn't have to ask what was up. He just said, "I'll be right there," and he arrived a few minutes later.

Bob was beside himself with excitement—the mare had been returned to the pasture! He had gathered her up and put her in a stall pen. He wasn't taking any chances with her.

Poppy didn't look so good. She was about 200 pounds lighter and had a large gash high on her left hind leg. As you might imagine, she was not acting quite herself either. She had dirt in her hooves that did not match soil in the pasture or the surrounding area. The hair on her face was worn away from wearing too tight of a halter, apparently having been tied up in a confined area. She looked rough. Spots of her hide were worn and she had sores on her sides.

"Have you called Troy?" Pops asked.

"He's already on his way," Bob responded. "The minute I told him the news, he was in his truck and headed this way. He'll be here in

"Beast of Burden"

about two hours I figure."

Troy showed up in a less than two hours. When he drove up and got out of his truck, he looked cautiously optimistic. Bob had warned him that she looked a little rough. Troy went straight to doctoring her, then loaded her in the trailer and hauled her up to Idaho be with her teammate, Tally.

It took many months, but Poppy mostly recovered and ended up hitched with Tally again, leading the eight-horse rig. To this day,

"Bridle Horse"

they don't know who stole her, where she was kept, or why she was taken. Everyone was just happy and relieved that she was returned.

Tally and Poppy were back together and completed one critical lead team. Cooper's Christmas spurs were also again fitted with their original pair of matching rowels. Both were rejoined and made a powerful reminder to always keep hope alive and ride tall in the saddle no matter how overwhelming the obstacles at the moment may appear.

"Herd Boss"

19. Ridin' for the Brand

Since being reunited, Cooper and those jingling spurs with their spinning rowels spent many hours on horseback, handling cattle, swinging a rope, and basically honing cowboy skills.

For all of Coop's youth, his family lived in a very special place. One that offered more than most people have a chance to enjoy, that is, when it comes to cowboyin'. Yet they were ever thinking of exploring new places, those elusive greener pastures.

Now that Levi had branched out from the little family tree, he was living in Idaho. He was building a name for himself as an up-and-coming buckaroo saddle maker. He was riding new ranges and continuing to make the generations proud.

Isaac announced, "I'm gettin' itchy to try something like Levi is doing. And I want to cowboy on a big cow outfit, you know. If I could do anything I wanted to do, that'd be it."

Cooper added, "And I want to ride herd alongside an old timey chuck wagon and be driving the teams, too."

"That's what I'm talking about," Isaac agreed.

"But it has to be a beautiful place surrounded by mountains and lots of space! We have it pretty good here so I'm not about to go to a place that isn't pretty to look at," Momma K, always the realist, added her concerns.

Annie just wanted the whole family to stay in one place, have fun, and work together.

Coop suggested, "What about that ranch in Wyoming that Levi worked on last year?"

Isaac piped up, "Yeah that would be cool. Maybe Levi could come visit us while we're there and maybe even help us, if he wanted."

And Pops thought, I'd just like to try some place new. We live in a great place alright, but I am curious to see what else is out there.

As Isaac, Annie, Cooper, Momma K, and Pops sat together and entertained ideas, they started to play the "What if" game, "What if we could go anywhere that we wanted? What if we could do anything we wanted?" etc. They had fun scheming and dreaming, but Pops felt like it was time to make it really happen.

They spent the next winter looking over and exploring various ranches that they could work on the following summer. Through a series of phone calls and talks with friends, Isaac, Cooper, their mother, and Pops got hired to cowboy on one of the largest cattle ranches in the country.

When it was a done deal, Pops let the kids in on the news, "Guess what, boys? We got the job!"

"Really? When do we start? Let's go now! Why do we have to wait? What do they want us to bring?" They let loose with a flurry of excited questions, "Did we really get hired on the Padlock Ranch, where Levi was?"

"Yes, the same one that Levi worked on."

"What all will we be doin'?" they wanted to know.

"For the time bein' our job is a seasonal one. Along with cowboyin' on the Ash Creek division of the ranch, we are to live in the lodge. While we're there, we'll accommodate guests who are scheduled to come participate in their Cowboy School."

"We don't care what we're doin', we're just ready to go."

The Padlock Ranch covered nearly half a million acres that straddled the Wyoming-Montana border, headquartered near the town of Sheridan. It was a vast and diverse landscape ranging from high pine-covered rocky peaks of the Big Horn Mountains to the wide-open grassy plains that ran as far north as Billings, Montana. Many rivers, streams, and a network of two-track roads crisscrossed the most beautiful land that ever God created. The ranch ran anywhere from 15,000 to 18,000 Angus cow-calf pairs, another 400 head of bulls, several hundred head of steers, and 2,300 replacement heifers at any one time.

To cover the ranch and do the daily cattle work, Padlock kept a remuda of nearly 100 head of saddle horses. In times past, all the winter feeding and much of the day-to-day draft work was done with Percheron draft teams, yet only one of the old teams was still on the ranch.

When spring was close, the family packed up and moved north to their new home in Wyoming, but there was a little sadness. Everyone except Annie was going, even though she was the one who just wanted them all to stay together. It didn't seem fair, but Annie was tough. She was willing to stay behind and look after the homestead. The growing pains of a family can be rough.

"Don't you forget me!" she teased as they were leaving. "I will be up to visit every chance I get. I love you!" She smiled as they waved goodbye. Annie had some college and work commitments that also kept her behind. Luckily, she was able to visit a few times.

Arriving in early spring, it was calving season and this required daily riding through the herd, checking for new or sick calves, and any other kind of trouble. They took their orders from Jesse, the same cow boss that Levi had worked for. It was an incredibly cold and rainy spring, flooding the creeks and rivers, washing out bridges, creating boggy conditions, and heightening the potential for shivering, sick calves. Sometimes, after riding all day in those hard-driving rainstorms, and even with a full slicker, good hat, and gloves, Pops thought he was going to freeze half to death. Somehow they made it sloshing out the other side of the rains smiling all the while because they were living the life of a cowboy, just livin' the dream.

As soon as most of the calves were on the ground and up on their feet, branding time started. Branding on the Padlock was done the original cowboy way, out on the range. Catch pens were set up and the chuck wagon was pulled to the same location. Then cattle

in the nearby area were driven to the temporary pens and sorted.

As big as the ranch was, the cattle had to be worked in many different and distant pastures rather than permanent corrals in a central location. Transporting so many cattle to one spot to treat them would be a logistical nightmare besides extremely time-consuming and, more importantly, too stressful on the cattle.

"Do you think we're ready for the brandin' tomorrow?" Pops asked Jesse. "We have some Cowboy School students who are anxious to see how it all works. They also want to be involved as much as possible."

"Oh yeah, we're ready. We have a great crew," Jesse said with confidence.

"Levi is coming to help. He'll be here later tonight. He didn't want to miss out on anything, you know," Pops told Jesse.

"It'll be good to see him. He's good help—at least he was last year. How's his saddle making comin'?" Jesse inquired.

"You know the first thing he did when he got a chance was he built himself a saddle. I think you'll like seein' it," Pops couldn't help but brag on him a little.

"I'm sure I will," Jesse agreed.

"Don't let on anything to Isaac when he rides in tonight, but just between me and you, Levi has been moonlightin' and he's built Isaac a new saddle, too. He's going to surprise him with it when he gets here. It is going to be a Hamley Daisy. It's a traditional design that has its origins in Oregon."

"Oh yeah, I know that design," Jesse said. "A cowboy can't get a better surprise than that."

"I'll let you know how it goes. He might be so excited that you may hear about it clear down here at your house."

"I'll be listenin'."

Levi arrived just before Isaac rode in from the "Upper Fifty" pasture. He had Annie with him, what a surprise! They propped the new saddle up on some chairs just inside the front door. Momma K orchestrated it all.

Isaac, tired from a long day, came dragging in. The saddle was the first thing he saw. "Surprise!" they all shouted.

Like Jesse said, "At this point in his life there's nothin' better that a cowboy can receive than a custom built saddle."

Pops thought, there's sure nothing wrong with having your brother build it for you either. How can it get any better than that?

When Isaac saw the saddle and realized who it was for, he let out a "Whoop" that all could hear. "A full stamped Hamley Daisy, that's so cool!" There were pats on the back and hugs all around, what a deal.

"Hi Annie," in his excitement Isaac remembered to say.

At the barn the next morning Jesse said to Isaac, "I heard you got a new saddle," he winked.

"Yeah I did. And it's way cool." Isaac was beaming.

Jesse set to work and got the crew organized. With the formalities out of the way, they mounted and lined out. "Who is riding that squeaky saddle?" some smart guy was heard to say. They made a wide circle and gathered about 150 pair of cows and calves into a grassy meadow, a pasture called Dan's.

Pops commented, "Never did a branding crew look so good."

The crew consisted of Jesse and his daughter Hanna, her friend Reata from the Houlihan Ranch, Isaac, Cooper, Annie, and Levi. To round out the bunch there was Momma K, Pops, and some other hands from other camps on the ranch and a couple of wide-eyed guests. They all took turns doing most every critical task.

Three or four would be on horseback and ease into the herd, keeping them as quiet as possible. They'd carefully rope a calf by the heels, then slide it out of the mob to the waiting ground crew (the pasture paramedics). A flurry of doctoring, marking, tagging, branding, dehorning, and health maintenance procedures would be done. From the time the calf was roped until the time it was turned loose averaged about two minutes. The process was very skilled, and it had to be done efficiently so the calves could be quickly returned to their mothers. When the cattle handling was done with finesse, it looked good and it just felt right.

Branding is typically an annual highlight on ranches. Cowboys use the roping skills they've perfected over the winter and show off any new gear they may have, including their handy broke horses. It's also a time that neighboring ranchers and cowhands travel to help each other, a time for reunions, comradery, telling stories, and celebrating spring and new life in the herds. It is a good time.

Nearly 13,000 calves were branded on the Padlock that year. With all that practice, Isaac, Cooper, and Levi had gotten pretty handy with their ropes. A true cowhand takes great

pride in his work, the horses he rides, the stock he handles, the land he lives on, and the brand he rides for.

As the long days of summer stretched on, Cooper carved out a little spare time in the evenings. He inquired at the ranch headquarters about the last remaining draft team on the ranch and learned that there was some interest in reviving them and taking them out of retirement.

"I'd be happy to get them in shape so we could use them at the lodge!" he willingly offered.

Buck and Kino were a well-seasoned team of Belgian horses. Due to modern machinery, a changing style of working cattle, and different philosophies in ranching, they had been laid off work

for several years. To be used, they needed a good deal of tuning up. With a new set of shoes, several sessions in the harness, and the loss of many extra pounds, Buck and Kino were back in shape and willing to work.

After regular work hours someone would ask, "Where is Cooper?"

"I'm sure he's down with those horses again," another would respond.

Coop would brush them and do their tails in all sorts of fancy braids. Besides driving great, in no time he had them looking really good, too. The pair pulled logs for the fire and towed the hayrack and salt wagon. They seemed to be happy to be back in the harness. Having them working around the yards restored an authentic flavor to the ranch. The guests loved to watch them pull and they took turns riding in the hay-wagon. It also offered a good experience and some real responsibility for Cooper.

The dream life was going along great. What more adventure could anyone ask for? One should know better than to think a question like that.

On a particularly nice evening late into the summer, Cooper came in from working. He had been riding on a group of 250 head of cows with calves. The pasture he was riding was about 20 miles from the house besides the 12 miles of dirt road he had to travel before he got to the pavement. He then traveled under one freeway and along a couple of other paved roads. This offered a lot of time for him to think and observe as he drove.

As he was driving, he came across what looked like a stray dog. He stopped and called to it. Sheepishly limping, it wagged its way over to him. "Are you hurt? Here let me help you. Do you want to get in the truck? Up we go, just sit there on the floor, I'll take care of you." He picked it up in what appeared to be the middle of nowhere. The dog had been injured and was hopping on three legs.

"Look what I found. Can I keep him?" Coop asked Pops. He then explained the circumstances in which he found the dog.

"The dog seems fine enough to be around, but does he know

anything about working cattle, you know, can he earn his keep?" Pops prodded.

Momma K offered a different concern, "This dog is too well mannered. I think he's someone's pet and they'll surely be missing him by now. You'd better put up some postings and see if you can find his real home."

Cooper did not want to hear that, saying, "But I found him in the middle of nowhere. Somebody must have just abandoned him on the highway, so they must not have wanted him."

Momma K encouraged him to do the right thing and try to find the dog's owner. She reminded him, "I remember how upset we were when we thought we lost Belle a couple of times and you know you'd feel really bad if it was your dog was missing then come to find out someone else had him the whole time. Remember how good you felt when your spur rowel was found?"

He reluctantly contacted the animal shelter in Sheridan and left their phone number in case someone came looking for a lost dog.

They had that dog for about ten days and Cooper was feeling pretty confident that he had found another new friend that he'd keep for his very own. Then the dreaded phone call came. "Yes this is Cooper," hesitantly he spoke on. "Yeah, that sounds like the dog I picked up, but you better come out and take a look and make sure he's yours."

After searching the area and reading the posts, the rightful owners finally made a connection with Cooper. It was a happy reunion for a young girl and her favorite pet. Seeing the happiness, Cooper was glad that he had done the right thing, even though it hurt a little.

Pops said, "He just can't help himself when it comes to finding animals and bringing them home. At the same time, he learned how important it is to try to help them find where they really belong."

Momma K does it all

"All Business"

20. MOUSEY GREY

Several miles from the lodge, in the same direction that Cooper had picked up the stray dog, was a 2,500-acre pasture where many of the ranch's bulls were wintered. As the summer went on, most of the bulls were placed out with different bunches of cows to do their job. When there were just a few remaining bulls, a mousey gray pony showed up in the pasture. It seemed quite independent roaming the large pasture, unconcerned with either the bulls or that it was mostly alone. They watched that pony for nearly three months, thinking someone would surely come and claim it. But no one did. It just stayed there.

As they drove by the pasture one day, Cooper couldn't stay away from the pony any longer. "Dad, let's stop the truck and get a closer look at that pony, and see if we can get up to it. Come on!" he urged.

"There's no way we'll get next to that independent pony in that big old pasture on foot. Maybe if a guy was horseback or if he had a bucket of grain or something to chum him in with, then maybe you'd get a rope on him. We don't even have a rope or halter with us." Pops knew what he was talking about.

"What do you know? I just happen to have a bucket of grain and a halter and rope in the back of the truck," Coop spoke as if he was surprised by his own actions.

Pops knew he had been ambushed and there was no way out

other than to go prove that they couldn't get close to that pony. They stopped on the highway near the bull pasture. They got out and climbed over the fence. With the bucket of grain, Cooper approached the pony. As he got closer, it seemed almost happy to see them. They saw that it was a mare with quite nice conformation and a quiet, approachable attitude. She appeared to have strong dark hooves and her color was a beautiful dappled grey.

Cooper asked, "Can we keep her, Dad?" Where had Pops heard that phrase before?

"Well I don't know. She looks awful good to me and she seems very nice to be around, but we'd better make sure that she doesn't belong to someone around here first," Pops said cautiously. "You remember that dog situation, don't you?"

They contacted the management at Padlock, the local brand inspector, and other authorities to determine if the pony had been reported missing. She had not been reported. It appeared that no one wanted to claim her either. "Go figure," Pops said, "It looks like we are back in the pony business."

They hooked on to a trailer, loaded her up (with no trouble at all) and hauled her to the Houlihan ranch where Reata lived. Once there, they checked the pony over really well. Upon further inspection, they found a tattoo running up and down her neck hidden by her long mane, signifying that she was, at one time, a wild BLM mustang.

Annually, the government land managers round up wild mustangs, determine if they're in good health, and for a low maintenance fee, they offer them up for adoption. Unfortunately, new owners are not always prepared to keep a horse and deal with all that owning one entails. Sometimes an unattended pasture can serve as a place to abandon them. It looked like that's what had happened with this little mare.

They called the local brand inspector again and he came out to give official approval to claim her. He also determined her age. According to the wear on the pony's teeth, he estimated the mare to be about seven years old and in good health. With the proper paperwork done, they decided to give her a new life, a good home, and a new name, something like Grey Pony. Quite original. Oh well, it would work for the time being. But the Padlock did not want the pony kept near the lodge.

"We can keep her at our place," Reata offered.

"That sounds good to us," was the agreement, so arrangements were made to take her there. The little mare had found a great temporary home at the Houlihan Ranch.

This opened the door for more options. Because the lodge was so far from town and fall was coming on, Cooper needed to attend high school. So another offer was made. "Cooper can stay here, too. He can help around the ranch," Reata's mother suggested.

"That would be great. Are you sure it wouldn't be too much trouble?" Momma K said with appreciation. The mothers talked and sorted out the details and finalized the situation. Cooper stayed there to go to school.

Now that's good people that'll take in strays who bring more strays with 'em, Pops thought.

With a new pony to spend time with after school, Cooper and Reata hurried home each day to ride the little mare. On occasion, Isaac also went to ride. In no time at all, they had her doing all the things a ranch horse needs to do. They were doing an incredible job.

In the beginning, the little mare had a fear of ropes. When mustangs are rounded up, the foals are often roped and physically pulled away from their mothers. This tends to leave them feeling distrustful and anxious toward ropes. With time and constant reassurance, the little gray mare grew to understand she was in safe hands with her new friends. She began to trust and even work with the rope.

Pops phoned Cooper and asked, "How is the pony doing?" He had learned that she was willing and teachable. She was also old enough to be moved right into cow-work without concerns of her being hurt. She was smooth, flexible, and tough, with great endurance. In short order she became a good pony to rope from, and was turning into a pony that any little buckaroo would be proud to ride.

"Gracey is doin' real good," Coop responded.

"So Gracey is her name? How did that come about?" Pops wondered aloud.

"Well she is gray and she is kind of easy to teach stuff, so Gracey just seemed like the right fit for her. You know, it's sort of a combination of the two, and she needed a name anyway." That made perfect sense to Pops.

"I'm happy for all of you and Gracey. Keep up the good work," he encouraged.

The thought of that pony and her new name prompted him to reflect on another little cow horse from the past, a little gray named Smoky. What are the chances that Cooper, so many years and miles later and by the grace of God would be doing ranch work and riding a mousey gray mustang? And doing it all at the same age that Grandpa Eddy was riding his own Smoky mustang so long ago? Like Pops said many times, it seems like someone from the Big Ranch was continually watching out for Coop.

By cowboyin' in the northern area, the boys were fortunate to make a variety of new friends. They learned important ranching skills and they practiced and perfected many new lariat loops. When they felt sure of themselves, they entered  some local ranch roping competitions. Because of the generous instruction they received from top hands and daily practice on the open range, they were quickly advancing in their skills.

They competed in "The Northern Range Ranch Roping Association." Levi and Isaac did well enough to make it to the yearend finals held in Billings, Montana, a good time for all.

Late in the fall, Cooper and Momma K returned home from the Padlock while Isaac and Pops stayed another month or so to tie up the loose ends that go along with fall cow work. Even though they only stayed a little longer, it started to get a bit lonely way out there on Ash Creek. They spent the final days riding the ranges. They checked fences, looked for sick cattle, and made sure the fall water tanks hadn't dried up.

Pops said, "Those pastures are so vast that we should split up so we can cover more ground." Ten to twelve hours a day they'd ride then meet up and head back to camp. They were long days. If they had a day off, Isaac would make his way into the Houlihan ranch to meet up with friends. They always seemed to do some roping cattle or work with Gracey.

"Dad," Isaac said one morning, "Let's get out of here for a day or so."

"What do you have in mind?" Pops asked.

"Well, my friends from town and some of the guys from the ranch are headed up to Hardin to a big ranch rodeo. I think we should go, too. It would be fun."

Pops thought about it for a minute and considered what it would take to go all the way to Hardin, Montana. "I don't know. Do you think it would be worth our while? You know, going that far and not to mention all there is to do around here?"

Isaac didn't hesitate. "Yeah I do," was his quick response. "And besides, like you were just thinkin', there's endless work around here. Whether we work all the time or take a day off, there'll still be more work to do. Come on, let's go," he pushed.

Pops could see his point, so he offered, "You make all the arrangements and I'll finish up some things I've been doin' and then we'll go." Isaac was out the door and getting things ready before Pops even finished talking.

They found themselves three hours and 150 miles later sitting on some old wooden bleachers. The aged red and white paint was peeling and chipping. Some of the boards were sagging and bent, yet the place was clean, swept, and in pretty good shape for its age. Across the way, the bucking shoots and catch pens were of the same era. These were the grandstands at the fairgrounds in Hardin, Montana, a far cry from the Pineview Roundup, Pops thought.

Isaac made his way through the people and found his friends. Pops found a spot on the bleachers and just sat there taking it all in. The nostalgia was so thick in the air it could almost be cut with a knife. Food venders made their way up and down the grandstands shouting out their offerings, "Hotdogs! Hotdogs! Get your dogs! Popcorn! Fresh buttered popcorn, get it here! Ice cold pop! Ice cold pop!" It was all conveyed in old time paper bags and cups of the same red and white pattern as the bleachers.

The crowd wasn't a huge one and it was mostly local yet diverse. It was in the middle of the Crow Indian reservation and they were well-represented. Generally, they were all buckarooed up and looked more like cowboys than the cowboys did. They looked good in their flat-brimmed hats, wild rags, fancy shirts, and colorful well-worn chaps. And boy could they rope and ride.

A couple of Indian bronco riders put on a big show for the crowd. They burst out of the chutes riding high, whooping and hollering like they were on the war path. Their wild wooly fringed chaps were flappin' and dust was flyin'. Both were bare-chested and had long braids flinging about their heads. As their broncos started to buck out, they would grab their cowboy hats in one hand and go to fanning the horse's neck and head to get them to buck more. They were definitely crowd pleasers.

Area ranches were represented and those cowboys put on equally impressive shows in their own way. They demonstrated expert ranch roping skills, assimilating the doctoring of sick cattle on the open range. The stock saddle bronco riding paralleled old time cowboys bucking out wild horses, as it was an everyday job on the ranch. It was nothing like a typical modern rodeo. All the events showed stockmanship, ranch etiquette, teamwork and athletic abilities, and skills used in real ranch work like branding cattle, capturing and taming wild horses, etc.

Pops had been to a lot of rodeos and he had sat on many different grandstands. But as he sat there taking it all in, it was as if he was being transported to another time and place, not one where he'd necessarily been before. But at the same time, a place that he somehow knew.

Then it hit him, I am at the Will James memorial rodeo in Hardin, Montana. The same Will James who stomped these same grounds in the early 1900's, the one who wrote and illustrated many story books, several were made into movies. The stories that created the romantic images Pops dreamed about during his childhood, the ones that vividly told of the

"Whip & Spur"

Wild West, the mustangs on the range, and old time rodeos. They were all here being played out, right before him. And he was in the same landscape and location where they'd originally been written. He realized, this is why it all seemed so familiar. This was incredible.

Tales like "Smoky the Cow Horse," "Horses I've Known," "Cow Country," "Cowboy in the Making," and "The Lone Cowboy." The list goes on. All stories of cowboys riding tall in the saddle. It's because of these stories that he experienced so long ago that this was all so familiar to him. Here Pops was and his boy Isaac was roping in this memorial event. It doesn't get better than that, not in my book, he thought.

When the festivities were over, they made their way back to the ranch. As they were driving, Isaac fidgeted like he had something he wanted to say but didn't quite know how. Finally, he just spoke up.

"I'm staying here, Dad," he said kind of careful and planned out.

"What do you mean you're stayin' here?" Pops truly wasn't sure what he meant.

"I like it here in Sheridan. I think this is where I want to live. I don't want to go back. It's not that anything is bad back home, it's just that I like it here better. There's way more chances to cowboy around here and that's what I want to do."

"What's your plan?" Pops asked.

"Now that we're about done on the Padlock, I've already found me another job out on the Houlihan Ranch in Sheridan," he was resolute all right.

"Well, I can't say as I blame you for wanting to stay, it sounds good to me," Pops was understandably proud of him and more than a little jealous. First chance they got, Pops helped him settle into the bunkhouse at the Houlihan Ranch.

The owner of the Houlihan Ranch was a man named Mr. Brannaman, Reata's dad. He'd made quite a mark on the horse world by being a very successful horse trainer and clinician. Consequently, he spent a lot of time away from home, traveling from place to place, so Isaac was hired by Mary, Reata's mother, to take care of the ranch while Mr. Brannaman was on the road.

"What about a horse? What are you gonna do about a horse? Seems like a cowboy always needs a good horse or two," Pops asked.

"I was thinking if you don't need Pete this winter, maybe I could keep him here and I have Gracey. I need to keep working with her. She's comin' along really well so that's two." He had thought long and hard and had already sorted this out.

"What's the deal with Gracey? What have you three kids worked out?"

"Well it's like this, Gracey is still here at the Houlihan and you know, they're feedin' her and all. So how we worked it out's like this. Cooper, Reata, and I made an agreement. We all like to ride Gracey, I mean she took to cow work like a pig takes to mud. But still she's a pony and won't ever be able to go all day and compete with a big horse when it comes to big ranch working. As cute as she is, we figure that she should be easy to sell."

"So what's the final agreement that you all figured out?" Pops asked.

"Cooper captured the pony, I'll end up doin' most of the training on her, and Reata knows all the right people to show her to when it comes time to selling her. Once we move her, we'll split the money in thirds, and we'll all come out ahead."

"Sounds like quite a venture. I hope it all works out for the best," Pops said.

A few days later, Pops was to go back home to be with Momma K, Annie, and Cooper. As he drove away from the Houlihan ranch it hit him, one more fledgling had spread his wings and was taking flight. The nest was getting emptier all the time. The seasons were changing just like the weather.

Ultimately, after the pony was proven, the business trio was able to market her. It took a few months, but Gracey went to a good family back east and made some fortunate youngster very happy. It proved to be a learning experience as well as a profitable venture for them. It is great to put together a good finished horse to have for oneself, but sometimes it's greater to provide that for someone else. Gracey was doing very well in her new home. But doing well and making another little feller happy at the same time, that's the best.

Having two critter friends come and go so quickly fueled Cooper's desire to scoop up another one. Once he returned home, he could not be still. He searched the want ads and found an Australian shepherd puppy, a male, beautiful blue merle with copper and white trim, just like old Belle. Coop named the pup after one of Belle's best sons, Stone. He sure knows how to pick 'em, Pops thought to himself.

"Spring Shade"

"Shaggy"

21. EQUINE LIFEGUARD

After a long winter, they always looked forward to a nice warm spring, which typically leads to an equally fine summer. The 29th of June was one of those pleasant, warm evenings. Pops was out at the tack shed when Cooper called from the house, "Pops, hey Pops it's here!" There was obvious excitement in his voice.

Pops hurried to the house to learn what was going on. "What's here?" he asked.

"A man from the Parry Ranch called and said one of our mares has foaled!"

Pops had two mares ready to foal at any time. They were in a pasture called "Spring Creek Pasture" about a mile upstream, east of their place near the Parry Ranch. The pasture was named Spring Creek because there is a prolific year round, crystal clear spring that bubbles up right out of the ground. From the spot where the spring surfaces until about 30 feet beyond, it goes from nothing to a full-fledged, 15-foot-wide creek a foot deep and flowing west. Lady, a sorrel mare, was due to foal first and Karla, a pretty little bay mare, was due soon after.

"Which one did he say? Which one of the mares has foaled?" Pops asked.

"He just said the bay mare. Karla had a baby! Dad, we have to go see it! Come on let's go," Cooper was so excited.

Considering that Karla was due second, Pops was thinking things like, maybe the caller didn't know for sure what he was seeing. It is starting to get dark or maybe he can't tell color. If it is Karla, I hope nothing is wrong, because there was a real reason to suspect something could go wrong for her.

"Let's go see," Pops said with those questions in his thoughts.

Momma K, Annie, Cooper, and Pops jumped in the truck. Pops' mind was racing as they headed for the pasture to see the new surprise. As they pulled into the field with the mares, they could see the mare and foal at the far end of the pasture. The foal was already up on its feet and sure enough it was Karla who had foaled. She had a beautiful little bay filly and it showed hints that it could turn roan.

They approached and upon further inspection, they were happy to find that the filly and her mother were in fine shape. Karla was a little

agitated with the human visitors, but that's to be expected of a first-time mother. They sat down in the grass and spent an hour or so just watching the wobbly little filly move about, nurse, and interact with her mother. Lady, respectfully, stayed a distance away, giving Karla her space. Mother and foal hovered near the head of the spring.

As they watched this new miracle before them, Pops glanced at the nearby spring bubbling up. He thought to himself how the spring itself also represented the miracle of life. And he could not help but reflect on the episode that had happened just two months earlier, one mile downstream on this same, life-giving creek.

"Horse Whisperer"

Pops was taking advantage of the nice April weather and getting some spring cleaning done around the tack shed. At the same time, he had left the gate open to allow Lady, Karla, and Pete to leave the corral and feed on the new grasses on the hill. Things could not have been nicer or any calmer, a lazy spring day.

As they meandered about, Pops watched Lady. She looked so uncomfortable as she was so obviously pregnant. The previous summer while on the Padlock, Pops had both mares bred. The mares were getting some age on them and neither one had ever had a foal. So Pops didn't know how either one would look when pregnant. Karla, who they also hoped was bred, certainly did not have the look of being in foal as much as Lady did. But her due date was a little after Lady's so if she was in foal Pops assumed that she had a body type that didn't show as much.

There was a pasture on the other side of Spring Creek. It was in the creek's flood plain so it could only be used later in the summer after the spring waters had subsided. The gate into that pasture was right in the low point of the creek bed. In high water, about 200 yards of the barbwire fence including the gate was not visible. It was under several feet of water. This is that same flooded creek where Cooper had gone coot diving in years past.

After an hour or two of grazing, the horses had made their way down to the water's edge, near where Stone was playing. Now they were standing ankle deep, drinking, and just being content. About that time, Stone romped down to see what the horses were up to.

He was not in pursuit or barking to be mean, he was just showing up to say hi. The horses must have been far away in their minds because the motion of the bounding dog was just enough to spook them forward into the water. Stone apparently saw it as a friendly game and followed after. The horses were soon belly deep in the water and it was rising fast.

Pops' heart sank. He could see exactly what was happening but was not sure how to stop them. He called Stone back and put him in his pen. By this time the horses were deep enough to be swimming, just their heads, necks, and withers were showing above the water's surface. They swam a wide circle then moved upstream. They were headed for the familiar pasture on the other side of Spring Creek with Pete leading the way. If they swam as far as the creek bed before turning upstream, the water might be deep enough that they could clear the submerged wire fence. Obviously they couldn't see the fence, but Pops could tell that the horses were turning too soon.

Pops ran down the fence line waving his arms in hopes of getting them to turn back. He knew if they swam into that fence it would be sure disaster. They were not in a panic or on a runaway, but they were traveling with a mission to get somewhere, the pasture on the other side.

"Pete"

Pete hit the submerged fence first. It got his attention. He rolled back and crashed into his sister Lady who was close behind him. They floundered and splashed about, but they were able to keep their heads above water and luckily found their way to a shallow spot with enough footing that they could raise themselves out of the water and take a rest.

By this time, Pops was waist deep in the flood and making his way down the fence. He was able to make enough commotion to get those two to turn back and head toward home. Karla, on the other hand, had swum out just a little farther than Pete and Lady. Pops could tell she was directly over the fence when she realized that her herd had turned back. Out of instinct to stay together, she tried to turn around.

In doing so, she sank a little lower in the water. Pops felt helpless as her beautiful eyes went wide. She started to panic. She was frantically swimming to save her life yet she was not moving. He knew then that she was tangled in the submerged wire fence.

Annie and Cooper were at school. Momma K was way up at the house. Pops called out to her for help just in case she might hear him, but he knew it was futile. She was too far away. He continued to approach Karla, not knowing what he was going to do. If he got too close, out of desperation she would try to climb on top of Pops just to save herself. But he had to do something. He made his way down the fence. By the time he got to her, the water was up to Pops' ears. He had to keep his head tipped back in order to breathe.

Karla was getting exhausted and starting to quit. As Pops reached her, he could tell she sensed that he intended to help and he believed she was starting to go into shock from the exhaustion. He also had no idea how tangled she was or what kind of injuries she may have from the rusty barbwire fence. At this point, he could see no blood coming to the water's surface, but her stomach had emptied out from her stress.

Pops finally got close enough to lift her head. She could not reach the bottom without going under water and like Pops thought, she was starting to quit. Pops just stood there on his tiptoes and held her nose above the water.

Now Pops and Karla had been together in the water for several minutes and from time to time she would give a burst of energy and try to break free of the wire doom that held her. As she did this, Pops would give it everything he had to roll her onto her back in hopes that she might thrash free. They were both getting tired. Pops was constantly concerned of her potential injuries and also keeping himself free from getting tangled between her and the fence wire. He tried to think of a way out of this mess—a plan of escape.

Momma K was too far away to hear him, but Pops continued to call out. What to do? He had no tools with him to cut the wire. He could not afford to let her head go long enough to swim down and try to free her legs from the wire with his bare hands. They were in a real fix!

After several more minutes of this, Pops noticed a fisherman in a float tube about 50 yards downstream. Pops hollered to him, "Hey can you help me?" The fisherman hesitantly responded as he approached, but he didn't look too sure. Pops knew that the fisherman was looking at this crazy scene and saying to himself. I just wanted a quiet day of fishing, not to get caught up in a mess like this. As he got closer, Pops asked if he had any tools, pliers, fence cutters, jack hammer, backhoe etc. He said he had nothing. Pops thought, that's odd for a fisherman to have no tools, but at least there was someone to talk to. Pops asked if he would run (and he meant run!) up to the house and get Momma K and some tools. He was willing and ran toward the house.

Pops tried to encourage him to hurry and muttered under his breath, "I don't think he realizes how serious this is." Pops had now been in the water for about twenty minutes and was starting to get cold. He thought of Cooper again, how he had almost frozen in this same water some years before. Soon the fisherman and Momma K returned, but the fisherman had not quite communicated how serious the dilemma was so they didn't have any tools with them. Pops told Momma K to go get some long-handled tree loppers and wire cutters. It was several more minutes before she returned again. Now Karla was just closing her eyes and hanging in the water while Pops held her nose up.

Momma K made her way down the fence line with the tools. As

she reached Pops, he had her balance herself on the fence. She was not tall enough to reach the bottom, keep her head above water, and hold Karla's head up, too. Once she was in position, Pops cautioned her, "No matter what happens, do not allow yourself to get tangled up with the horse or the fence. We have one disaster here; we do not need a bigger one!"

Pops made his way to Karla's rear end because it was obvious that her hind legs were the ones that were tangled. By now they had been in the water for the better part of an hour. Pops carefully made his way down the horse's legs to the fence wires. The water was murky from all the commotion so Pops couldn't see anything. He had to blindly feel his way along.

Once he got hold of the wire and guided the loppers into position, Pops started cutting every wire that he could feel. All at once, Karla felt a renewed ambition and started to scramble. Pops pushed himself free of her flailing legs and she broke free.

Pops told Momma K, "Do whatever you have to do to keep Karla moving away from the fence, and don't let her get tangled again." Momma K did her job and Karla got herself to shallow water and stood long enough to take a rest then shakily made her way to dry ground. As she struggled out of the water she was wobbly legged and exhausted, but amazingly she had very few wounds. Mostly just one leg was sawed up from thrashing in the tangled wire, along with a few other scratches and scrapes.

Momma K doctored Karla immediately and she healed well. But the question now was, if she is pregnant, is the foal ok? That kind of stress and being submerged in such dirty water could easily cause a mare to abort a foal, Pops thought. If it did not go that far, it sure could cause serious damage to the unborn baby.

For the next couple of months, they watched her closely and hoped and prayed for the best. Apparently it worked. They had a brand new, healthy filly. Once again thanks to the Big Ranch.

By the time they were leaving the pasture from seeing the new baby, it was getting dark. Pops had lived in that valley for nearly 50 years and there had only been three occasions when he had seen fireflies. As they walked through the tall grass, there were many fireflies glowing on the grass tops. Momma K thought, "Fire Fly," that is a good name for this little survivor and we can call her Fly for short.

"Scarlett"

"Wrapped in Glory"

22. PATRIOTS

Between the time that Pops was lifeguard for Karla and when Fly was born, a good friend had called and asked if he was interested in buying a horse. That's all we need is another horse, Pops thought. On the other hand, they were always in the market for the right horse at the right price. So he said, "Well it depends. What have you got?"

She went on to describe the horse that she wanted to sell. "He's a beautiful, long legged bay gelding—a quarter horse."

Pops again thought to himself, they're all beautiful when they're for sale.

The owner explained, "He can be a dream to ride, but he has gotten sort of barn sour. You know, he wants to bolt for home from time to time and now I'm a little scared to ride him. Like I said, he is very tall and I cannot afford to take a fall, if you know what I mean. I guess he's got me a little buffaloed. Also, I just don't have the time to put into him that he needs," she said.

"How old is he? Is he papered, has he had any experience on cattle?" Pops asked all the usual questions that he would ask to figure out if he was interested in a horse or not. She replied with a discouraging string of no's. There was one plus—he was papered.

Because she was an old friend, Pops told her he'd come take a look at the horse and let her know if he was interested. Cooper and Pops drove out there the next day to take a look. He was a beauty all right, dark blood bay, sharp looking head, good withers, apparently sound, and solid legs and feet. But he was eleven years old, skittish, and knew relatively nothing about working cattle, so Pops was a little skeptical and didn't act too interested. His friend said, "How about you just take him home and try him out. If you decide you like him, you can have him for $500." At that offer, Pops didn't see how they could go wrong.

They got him home that same day and Cooper went right to work riding him. Coop was anxious to see if he would make a cow horse. If so, he would be back in the horse business. If he could get to where he could ranch rope off of him and make him good around crowds and commotion, he might just be worth having, or selling?

Pops asked Coop "What do think we ought to call him?"

"Boone," Coop said.

"Does that have some kind of meaning, like Daniel Boone or somethin'?" Pops wondered.

"No, I just think it sounds good and I kind of like it," Coop replied.

"Well then Boone it is," Pops confirmed.

The Fourth of July had always been a special gathering time for the family. Several years before, they had turned the production of the little rodeo over to a committee. For the last few years, Cooper had taken a real interest in helping to make the day more memorable for the community. He had been organizing a morning flag raising and a retiring of the colors later in the evening. With Cooper, it had to be an all-out event and must involve horses. When he first decided to do the program, Pops asked, "What's your plan and how can we help you get it done?"

He'd been pondering it for some time. He laid it all out for Pops. "I want to have a flag pole out in the middle of the park somehow so everyone will be able to see. I want it to be a big deal."

"I can help you with that. We can use a hay wagon for a stage and mount a flag pole in the middle of it. What's your plan to get the folded flag to the stage and who is going to raise it?" Pops asked.

Cooper described his plan in detail. "I'm going to have three horse riders and they'll be dressed like Cavalry Soldiers. They'll start out ridin' on the opposite side of the park from the stage. The one in the middle will be holding a folded American flag. The riders on either side will be carrying flags on eight foot poles."

Pops said, "That sounds good. What then?"

"Then I want a real loud sound system to start playing a song called, "Until the Last Shot's Fired" by Trace Atkins and backed up by the Marines Military Choir. That'll get everyone's attention.

"Patriots"

While the song is playing, the two riders with the flag poles will circle the whole park. You know, ride right through the crowd. Then come all the way back along either side of the rider holdin' the folded flag. Then, they'll ride straight across the park through the crowds to the stage."

"We can dress up the wagon with some red white and blue bunting, that way it'll look more like a stage than an old wagon," Pops offered.

"That'll be good," he said, liking that idea.

"Well, Coop, it sounds like you've thought this all out. That's good, what then? Will the rider get off and raise the flag?"

"No," he said, "this is where it gets good. All along I want some old veterans to be standing on the stage at attention waitin' for the folded flag. The rider'll get off and hand the flag to one of the veterans, then he will raise it and lead the entire town in the Pledge of Allegiance."

"Sounds great," this time Pops was sure he must be done.

"Yeah but that's not all. Then one of 'em is going to give a short patriotic talk. Then it'll be done and the rest of the day can get started."

"Who are the riders going' to be and what horses are you thinkin' of using?"

"Well, I thought me, you, and Levi could be the riders," he said.

"What horses are you thinkin' of because you know they've got to be good ones. There'll be a lot of people and commotion, and we cannot afford to have a wreck," Pops said.

He had also been contemplating this. Coop said, "I want the whole event to look really good so I thought Levi could bring his new black horse. You could ride that bay colt that you're training and I'll ride Boone. Can you picture it? A black flanked by two bays?"

Pops said with concern, "You know none of those horses have done anything like this and we don't have much time. Do you think they can be ready and safe?"

"Red, White and You"

"Don't worry. We'll practice and it'll all be good. You'll see," Coop assured him.

Don't worry? After all these years of horses and kids, I'm all practiced up at worrying, Pops thought to himself.

Worry was exchanged for work. Coop spent many hours waving flags and ropes around Boone and riding him through town in the middle of cars and groups of people. Boone was jittery at first and pretty nervous about the commotion, but Cooper was persistent. He practiced like it was the real thing until the big horse was totally comfortable carrying a flag over his head in the middle of a strange environment.

When the time came for the event, they were ready. Coop had wanted it to be good and he ended up getting much more. It was a moving experience for all. The crowd was silent, respectful, and honored the occasion, and the retiring of the colors was just as amazing. As they rode along and presented those flags with the music playing and the crowd at attention, it was a good feeling and Coop was riding mighty tall. It was the beginning of a great tradition. At eighteen years old, Coop could be proud of all he was doing.

The previous owner of Boone was in the crowd and approached them after. She said, "I can't believe you had that horse carryin' the flag on a pole in the middle of all those people and only a few weeks ago he'd never done anything like that. He looked so good. I am glad he found a good home and a job to do."

The way Pops figured, there's nothing wrong when good things come along, and especially when it happens in bunches.

Pops was still up at the park helping with the festivities when Momma K came rushing up with excitement in her voice. She announced, "Lady has foaled!"

The news caught Pops by surprise. He was so consumed helping Cooper that he had forgotten all about Lady and her time getting close. "Did they say what it looked like?" Pops inquired.

"It's a little sorrel, stud colt, with a white star on his forehead. That's all they said," she shrugged. Pops thought, A star on his forehead. How appropriate on the Fourth of July. He dropped what he was doing and they hurried up to the pasture to see the new foal. After a thorough inspection, Pops was happy to find the foal healthy, straight and sound, a real Yankee Doodle Dandy.

"What are we gonna name him?" Momma K asked.

"I think a fitting name for an Independence Day foal would be something like 'Patriot'," Pops said.

"I like it. We can call him Pate for short."

"Pate it is," Pops agreed. Considering Pops' habit of naming the foals in connection with things happening at the time they were being born, it's fortunate that there wasn't a screaming cat or a bloated cow or, heaven forbid, a squatting dog nearby. Just sayin'.

He turned to Momma K and said, "You know, I just thought of something else." He paused to reflect and then continued, "That little feller is the great grandson of Lily. I like that we're keeping her legacy going."

"The babysitter lives on," Momma K added as they walked hand in hand.

"Bridled Passions"

23. GOOD NEWS

Around Pops and Momma K's house, good news is always welcome. Cowboy philosophy says, "If you want to get to the top of the pile in life you're gonna have to do a lot of clawin' and climbin'." Another adage goes, "It's not what you know but who you know." These claims seem to be generally true. The same kind of thinking reminds us that when it's all said and done, "What really counts in the end is the type of person that you have become, when you get to where it is you're goin'."

Isaac definitely liked being on the Houlihan Ranch, who wouldn't? When he had been there for some time, he phoned home.

"Dad, guess what happened?" he said.

Pops could hardly guess. The question was wide open, but from the enthusiasm in Isaac's voice it must have been something good, or at least Pops hoped it was.

"I have no idea. Tell me what's up." Pops tried to equal Isaac's excitement.

Isaac went on, "Well you know I've been here at the Houlihan, helpin' out because Buck is gone a lot. But for the last few weeks he's been around. He's takin' a short break from bein' on the road and while he's been here we've got to know each other a bit. We've done a bunch of work together."

"Like what?" Pops encouraged.

"Well, like the other day we spent all day rounding up some wild wautusie cattle that a neighbor had turned out here on the Houlihan. We were able to herd some into the corrals, then we had to rope others and one old cow was so wild we even had to snare her in the trees to get her caught."

"What do you mean snare?" Pops asked.

"Well she was so wild we couldn't even get close to her. So we hung a big loop of rope in the trees where they hung low over the trail. Then we tied the other end of the rope to a nearby tree stump. Then we pushed her down the trail pretty fast, so she wouldn't notice the rope until she'd already put her head and big set of longhorns through the loop and it started to pull tight. Then we just rode our horses up and got the rope from the stump and towed her into the corral with the other cattle," Isaac explained.

"That sounds crafty," Pops responded.

"It wasn't perfect, but sometimes you do what you gotta do. I've learned a lot more about big loop roping and training horses, too. I can't hardly tell you all the fun stuff we've been doing."

Pops could not help but say, "We're so happy for you, and the experience you're gettin'. You know you couldn't get that just anywhere."

"But that's not all," he said. "Buck likes what I've been doin' around here and has offered me a job to go on the road with him when he goes back out. What do you think?"

"Sounds like somethin' you better jump on. Chances like that don't come around every lifetime," Pops encouraged.

"Oh, I will! And another thing, he's offered me a horse!"

"He gave you a horse? What do you mean?" Where is all this good news going to end? Pops wondered to himself.

"Well they raise a few horses here of a certain cow-horse breeding and with Buck gone a lot of the time, not all of the horses get as much use as they ought to. There's this one mare that Buck said I could have if I promised to train her and take care of her. They call her Willow. Maybe I'll breed her to one of the studs here one day and start a herd of my own."

"But why did he give her to you?" Pops probed.

"Like I said, Buck likes what I've been doin' here so he and Mary talked it over and decided that I should have her, that's all." It was as simple as that.

Pops was happy for him and his new horse, but much more, as a father, he was happy for the opportunities and the trust that had been placed in Isaac. Isaac is truly riding tall, he thought.

Isaac was hired to take care of most everything that Buck needed help with while he was traveling and instructing clinics. This was the greatest educational opportunity that any young hopeful horseman could ever have and Isaac was anxious to take full advantage of it. He hung on every word and applied all he learned to improve his stockmanship and horse-training skills.

After the excitement of learning about Isaac's good fortune, Pops' thoughts cleared and he said, "Sorry to change the subject, but did you hear about Annie's new gig?"

"I heard somethin' was up. What's the deal?"

"You remember Misty at the Western and Tack store in town? Well she pulled some strings with some people that she knows and put Annie in touch with the big wigs in the western clothing industry."

"How did that go?" Isaac asked

"To make a long story short, Annie is now a sales rep for Wrangler clothing and will be traveling and working all around the country for them."

Annie always wanted to do something big. She needed to make her own mark in the cowboy world, so to say. She had always worked hard at every job she had, whether it was selling sports equipment, health food marketing, cleaning houses, being a nanny, or manning the toll booth at the local boat dock. She always showed up and did her best. Now with a college degree in hand, an impressive resume, and the help of a good friend, she was career bound.

"She'll be puttin' her cowgirl fashion sense to good use," Pops said.

"Yeah, all those times she worried about how us boys looked when we went anywhere has paid off! That is so sweet she is going to do good. I hope she can get us all a good deal on pants and stuff," Isaac added.

"I'm sure she'll do what she can. Keep in touch with her in your travels. You might just cross paths like in Texas or Montana or somewhere."

They talked on. "Well now that it's mid-winter and since you're going to be gone most of the time, I better come get Pete and put him to use here."

"Yeah we won't be here much so Pete will just be turned out. You may as well come get him whenever you get a chance."

"I'll let you know when I can come. Remember to call Mom regularly while you're on the road. She lives to hear you kids' voices and know how you're doing and learn the good news," Pops reminded Isaac.

"I will," Isaac said.

"We'll talk to you later. Tell everyone 'Hi' at the Houlihan for us."

The fledglings are startin' to make their own way in this big old world. It's fun to see them soaring, Pops thought to himself.

If you feel too short with your feet stuck to the ground,
Then find a good pony to straddle.
This cowboy fact is easily found,
You're never so tall, as when you sit up in a saddle.

"Filly Gawkers"

"Sheer Cowboy"

24. Italian Buckaroo

"Guess who's comin' to see us?" Momma K teased.

"Is it somebody we know?" Pops asked.

"Well, they're from Italy."

"Oh I know, Francesco and Marianna!"

Francesco and his wife Marianna were a bubbly elder couple from Italy. While Pops and Momma K were on the Padlock, they came to stay at the lodge and they had all made a lasting connection.

"They sure took a liking to the boys, didn't they? When are they coming and how long are they staying?" Pops liked to get straight to the point.

"Just a few days. They are touring around the U.S. with some of their family and want to stop and see us before they fly back to Italy," she informed.

Once Francesco and Mariana got to Pops and Momma K's place, they had a great time renewing their friendships and took in some local sightseeing. When it was time for them to go, they were sad to leave.

At the end of their stay, Marianna approached Momma K and said, "Cooper can come go back to Italy with us, yes? We want him to come to our house, stay for two maybe three months and I teach him Italian to speak. He will have good time, yes?"

Cooper was within earshot and piped up, "Yeah, I want to go to Italy! Can I go, Mom?" Then turning to Pops, said with his puppy dog eyes, "Can I go?"

Whether to let him go or not was a difficult decision. On one hand it could be another great experience for him, on the other hand his mother was understandably nervous to let him go so far away. After some "behind the door" talks between Pops and Momma K, a plan was hatched. Pops sat Coop down and said, "We've decided you can go to Italy if you can come up with the money to pay your own way over and back."

"That's a Dandy idea," Coop muttered.

"What's that?" Pops said.

"Oh nothin'," Coop covered.

Their thinking was, if Coop wanted to go bad enough, he could figure out a way to come up with the money and prove himself mature enough to go. Knowing Cooper, Pops was not sure if it was proof of maturity or sheer stubbornness. Nonetheless, Coop figured out a way to raise the money and made it happen. A few weeks after Francesco and Marianna went back to Italy, Cooper followed.

When he first got to Italy, he kept in touch and every contact seemed to begin with, "How is Stone?"

A short time later, the phone rang again and with anticipation, Momma K answered. "Hello? Hi Cooper. Is everything okay, are you having fun?" she answered with her usual excitement when one of her kids called.

"It's okay," he replied with an unusual somberness in his voice.

"What's the matter, Coop? You don't sound very happy."

He explained, "Well, once I got here to Italy I was impressed with the country, the architecture, and all the beautiful scenery, but after a week the new sort of wore off. I hadn't thought about Francesco and Marianna being so much older than me and not having the same ideas

"Double Trouble"

of fun as I do." Coop was venting his misgivings. "After picking up rocks in their pasture, doin' yard work, cutting firewood, and a bunch of other household chores, I decided that maybe the trip wasn't worth the money. I started thinkin' I could have done this kind of stuff at home. It got old real fast." Obviously, he had hopes of a much more exciting adventure than he was having. He was homesick. He liked Francesco and Marianna very much and did not want to offend them, but maybe they had already lived out all their adventures. Now what was he going to do? The plan was for him to be there for two months, he'd only been there one week. This was lookin' to be a long two months! he thought.

In his temporary misery, he had also contacted Levi, Annie, and Isaac and shared his frustrations with them. When he next called to talk to Momma K, he sounded like he was at the end of his emotional rope. He took a big breath and said, "What if I just come home? I have lots of things that I could be doin' there."

Pops was reluctant, "You know, it cost you a lot of money to get over there. I think you ought to stick it out and make the best of it. Give it a chance. You may never go there again."

Uncertain, he said, "I'll give it a try and see if I can make it work, but I don't know."

If he'd only known the adventure that was waiting for him just around the corner.

A few weeks before Coop had gone to Italy, Isaac had become acquainted with another couple from Italy, Drew and Natalia. Drew operated a cattle ranch in the south of Italy called "The Silver Seal" and a business known as the "Rockin' A. N. Cow Camp." They instructed clinics throughout Western Europe, teaching the skills of the Buckaroo. They also promoted the European Ranch Roping Association or ERRA.

Isaac made the contact and was able to put them in touch with Cooper. What are brothers for? Drew offered to have Coop join them at a clinic they were teaching in a town near where Marianna lived. Surely this would help to cheer him up.

After the clinic, Coop immediately phoned home. "I have a chance to go ride and work cattle with Isaacs's friends here in Italy. Like I said before, I don't want to make Marianna feel bad, but I really want to go. What do you think I should do?"

He sounded like a whole different boy.

Pops and Momma K again were rightfully concerned because they had never met these people. "I know what you mean about Marianna feeling bad, but again, this sounds like a once in a lifetime opportunity. Let us know how we can help and what you decide," Momma K said.

On the heels of that conversation, another call came. It was Drew. In his broken English, he said, "Hi yah buddy this is Drew. We would like for Cooper to come for a visit and possibly stay with us, is this good?

He is good boy, and we take care of him good, is this good with you?"

Pops replied, "We appreciate your offer and hospitality, but are you sure it won't be too much trouble?"

"No, no it is good, he can be good help to us with teaching, he can be our real American cowboy, he is good cowboy and he can be big help," Drew told Pops.

Reassured that Cooper was going to be in good hand's, Pops consented, like he had much of a choice.

"I hope he can be good help to you and, again, we appreciate you takin' care of him for us. Thanks so much, we'll talk to you soon. And we hope to have you and your wife stay here at our place someday." They said their goodbyes. Pops and Momma K were more comfortable and felt like Coop was in a good place. Like a cat, there he was, dropped upside-down and landing on his feet again.

Coop's new friends took him to their place, a small town north of Milano, Italy. They put him in their bunkhouse and arranged a bridle horse for him to ride. They provided him with a long rope, gave him boots and a new flat hat, and hauled him all over Italy where he joined them in their ranch roping competitions.

Once Coop was back in the saddle, and sitting tall, he didn't seem to need to send messages home so often. Momma K hardly got a phone call after that, but when she did, it was usually to check on Stone. Funny how that works.

Pops knew Coop was surely going to run out of money. He had barely put together enough to simply get to Italy, let alone have funds to travel all around.

Coop finally called. "Hey how's it goin'?" Pops asked.

"I'm havin' a great time and they're treating me real good, but I'm kind of feeling bad, sort of like a free loader, you know what I mean?" he said sheepishly. "They keep tellin' me not to worry about it, but I just wish I had a little money so I could help out on little things like food and stuff when we're traveling."

"How can we help?" Pops prodded.

"Like I said, they're bein' way nice to me, and they're takin' me everywhere. But I'd feel better if I had some of my own money, to at least help pay my own way."

Not wanting to go back on their original deal, Pops said, "What do you think we ought to do?"

"I don't know," Coop said with some frustration in his voice.

Pops suggested, "You have this big gelding here. You bought him and now with all that you've done with him, he should be worth more than what you paid. Do you want me to see if I could sell him?"

Coop was a little reluctant. He'd grown a little fond of Boone. But he didn't know what else to do, so he agreed.

"But get as much as you can, he's worth it," he added.

"I'll see what I can do," Pops reassured him.

Pops immediately started to market the horse. He offered it for three times what Cooper had paid for him. In two days, he was sold. There were calls from as far as 200 miles away, yet they ended up selling the horse to a man just up the street.

They contacted Coop with the good news. Pops wired the money and Coop was back in the saddle again. From the little that they heard, it seemed like he was having the time of his life.

As the two-month mark approached, Coop called. Momma K answered and said, "Hi, Cooper, how ya doin'? What have you been doin'? Do you miss me? You've been there almost two months. Are you ready to come home?" She couldn't help herself.

He explained how he'd worked with the horses and dogs, and how he could now speak enough Italian to get by. "And best of all, I've been

able to rope and work cattle most every day." Then he said, "Things are great! That's what I'm callin' about." He took a confidence-building breath and said, "Can I stay here a little longer?"

"But I thought you'd be ready to come home, we miss you," she said.

"Well, yeah, but they're having the ranch ropin' finals and I'm doin' really good. I just want to stay a couple more weeks. What do you think? Like you said, I may never get over here again and I should make the most of it," he pled his case.

It did make a lot more sense to extend for a short while than to gear up and make a whole different trip over there later, so she gave in.

The day finally came to pick Coop up from the airport. He called ahead asking, "Will you bring Stone to the airport?"

Pops said, "No, you'll have to wait until we drive home, that dog won't want to ride that far in a car. Anyway, you'll see him soon enough."

As Pops, Momma K, Annie, and Isaac, who was home for a visit, drove the hour drive to the airport, there was much anticipation to see Cooper and hear how his trip was. At last, it was a happy reunion, hugs all around (Mom first, though).

Pops asked, "Where did you get that new buckle?"

"I won it! In the ERRA finals. It's the 'Top Hand' award. Pretty cool, huh?" Cooper was happy to let them know.

As they drove toward home, Pops thought to himself, top hand, go figure. Then he asked out loud, "What else did you do besides rope and ride while you were over there?"

"For a few days we rounded up wild horses on their ranch near the town of Tolfa. We gathered mobs of horses out of the foothills and pushed them onto a table top bluff overlooking the Mediterranean."

Cowboyin' on the Mediterranean Sea

"Wow!" Momma K said, as she sat next to Cooper.

"I have pictures, I will show them to you when we get home," Coop promised.

"Why did you gather them?" Annie, asked.

"They manage them for future ranch horses. We brought them into corrals and sorted 'em. We sent some to market, some needed to be doctored, and the mares were matched with a couple of Quarter horse and Thoroughbred stallions to improve their genetics. Then they were put into bands and turned back out on the range."

"That must have been beautiful," Momma K added.

"We were right above the port city of Civitavecchia, on the Italian west coast, and you're right, it was beautiful. The old stone buildings that have been standing there for centuries were like medieval castles that I would have dreamed of roaming when I was little knight."

Pops imagined, the little Knight of years ago, how he had dressed up Dandy to be a jousting horse. It all fit together in his mind.

Coop went on, "And you know, the horses that we were gathering are actual descendants from ancient abandoned war horses."

"Sounds romantic," Momma K said.

"What did they dress like?" The ever fashion-conscious Annie asked.

"Oh, you would have liked it. When they go to rope they tend to dress really, really nice. It's kind of show time, an expression of pride in themselves," Cooper said.

Isaac did his fair share of quizzing him about his new Italian hat and boots, and the horses and all of the gear they used.

They all wanted to learn about Italy, where he'd gone, what he'd done, and who all he'd met in his travels. So the questions kept coming.

Pops finally asked, "So was it worth it?

Coop gave him a puzzled look.

"Job is on the Line"

"You know, pickin' up rocks for Marianna? Bein' homesick, selling Boone to keep you funded?" Then with a glance in Momma K's direction, he said, "And you know, bein' away from all of us for several months?"

"It was so worth it I would do it again in a heartbeat. In fact, they have asked me to come back next year. Do you remember once a long time ago when you hauled me up on ol' Slick, in the saddle with you and told me all about ridin' tall?"

Pops did.

"Well, being able to do all the things that I've been able to do, including going to Italy, has helped me to understand what that all meant. So going over there all alone and stickin' it out, well, I think I was sorta ridin' tall in the saddle just like you told me to."

Italian Coop

Pops couldn't have been more proud. As they drove home and over the next several months, they heard many more stories of Cooper's Italian adventures. Once they got to the house, Stone was romping about, he was happy to see Coop.

Six weeks later, Cooper headed off to college. With all the kids off flying on their own wings, Momma K's little nest was pretty much empty. It was quiet around the place and time just slowed down. Life became a simple routine, no more carting after the kids like they had done for so many years with all of their activities and adventures. Pops' time was generally spent feeding horses, taking care of the place, and painting. After a while, they were getting used to the slower pace, maybe even liking it.

When Pops reminisces about the past, a flood of memories will wash over him. He considers how Cooper and the other kids have gotten to this point, especially at such young ages. They have obviously put their own ambitions out there and made things happen. But like the old saying goes, "It takes a village to raise a child." And the village has definitely done its part in the raising of these children.

Looking back, it's easy to forget specific days or exactly when things happened. But moments and experiences like these tales of Levi, Isaac, Cheyenne, and Cooper, along with their ponies of all sizes, will live and grow forever in their memories.

The invisible strands that tie generations together are continuing. They've been dallied up, strengthened, and no matter how they're stretched, will come full circle, like the closed loop of a carefully crafted four strand reata. Even when completed, the loop is ever expanding. There are always more coils to be added to include all who are willing to enjoy the life of a cowboy.

Their forefathers' love for horses has crossed time and generations to be permanently branded on their hearts, a powerful and binding union, and the glue that bonds families, generations, communities, and worlds together for always.

Their grandfathers are surely watching over them as they work with horses and learn the important skills of life such as hard work, integrity, patience, communication, and loyalty—the traits that eventually make a good little cowboy into a great man.

One who rides "Tall in the Saddle."

"Heart of a Cowboy"

25. DOG-GONE

"Why does it seem to be that it's always your best horse that goes lame, or your favorite dog that comes up missing?" Pops always said. "I can have an ill-tempered or ornery horse around for years and it'll never get hurt. At the same time, that horse never really makes a great mount but then again it isn't bad enough to just get rid of. Sort of like a sticky booger, you know one that you just can't shake loose of. Then it seems like when a real good horse comes along, one to be proud of and excited about, it'll go and get wire cut, or sored up, or founder, maybe get a fistula, or some other injury, that either lays 'um up for a while or even worse. Why do you think that is? It's somethin' to ponder."

When he went on like that, he was not necessarily talking to anyone in particular and he was never really expecting an answer. He was just speculating the concept. He would usually continue, "But when the good ones turn out, it's all worth it. I guess that's why we keep on tryin', you got to just keep on tryin'."

Time marches on, things come and things go, lessons are learned. A lot of water had crossed under the proverbial bridge, and seasons had rolled over and changed. Some years had gone down the road, and life for the family had simply gone on. Cooper had made a half-hearted stab at going to university and decided that it wasn't for him. He'd done a bunch more cowboyin' and he just happened to be passing through the old hometown. This time he was able to stay for a couple of days.

On his last afternoon at home, he, Pops, and Momma K were visiting as Coop sat stroking the ear of a curious looking, nearly all white dog, Gus. The dog was a border collie by breeding, but did not look like a traditional one. No fluffy, mid-length hair, no symmetrical black and white markings. He just had short, white hair with a few black dots on his ears, kind of like a young Dalmatian just coming into its spots.

"Where did Gus' mother come from again?" Momma K wondered as she looked down at him. She had bonded with Gus and had a real affection for him.

"Remember while I was away at school and I learned that Stone had come up missing?" Coop started to say.

Pops injected, "That was a shame, and he was gonna be a good one. You know there were a couple of other good dogs that came up missing around here about that same time from other peoples' places. Everybody thinks they were stolen. You know, by some passerby. You know what I always say...."

Momma K cut him off, "Yes we know what you always say, and you don't know that for sure, now let's get back to hearing about Gus."

"Still the same, if they'd have been Junker dogs nobody would've taken 'em." Pops retorted.

"Anyway, Cooper was reminding us where Gus' mother came from. Go on, Coop," Momma K prodded.

Drawn back into the conversation, Cooper continued, "While I was at school, a friend there heard about what happened to Stone and felt bad for me, so he gave Gus' mother to me. About that same time, I was just leavin' school to go up to Wyoming to ride some colts for a lady in Thermopolis. I took the dog with me and she came into heat while I was there, and a male dog on the ranch got to her. That's how we got Gus."

"It wasn't quite that simple," Momma K reminded him. "Meantime you'd put together another trip to Italy and went off and left the whelping to Pops and me. It's a good thing Belle was such a nice dog to be around." She stopped mid-thought, with a distant look in her eyes and momentarily considered her own words, then added, "Isn't it a strange coincidence that her name was Belle, just like our good old dog that about half-raised you when you were just a little boundary pushing boy, Coop?" Then with hesitation, she added, "I still miss her."

"There were only two pups, a traditional lookin' border collie pup and then a pure white one that had no traditional look about it. I was ready to get rid of it. I thought he looked just like a little white rat," Pops muttered.

"Now look what he's grown into. He's a dog to be proud of. Gus and me are bonded, ever since I saved his life from that black widow spider bite under his tail, I doctored him for weeks after the rest of you had given up on him. With herbs, my witch-doctoring and a little help from the Big Ranch, we saved his life. He loves me. Don't you Gus?" Momma K said as she reached down and lovingly scratched his head. Gus reacted with genuine affection, wagging his crooked tail.

"He looks more like a pit bull than a border collie," Pops added.

"Yeah, he's a good one," Coop agreed. "And he's tough as a pit bull, too, but he's smart as a collie dog. Did I tell you what happened a few weeks ago, when the cattle buyer from Cody came out to the ranch to look at our yearlings?"

"No. Did it have to do with Gus?" Momma K asked.

"Yeah, we had to sort through all of the cattle so the buyer could get a good look at 'em, usually that takes a set of corrals and a crew of hands to be done right. But we just went out in the big pastures and Gus did all the work for us. It was impressive. I'd have him

gather 'em in a big bunch, then I'd tell him to move 'em or cut some out so we could get a better look at 'em individually. Old Gus just kept workin' the whole time. At the end of the day, the cattle buyer asked if my dog was for sale. I told him yes, but only for the right price. I kind of thought he would drop it there, but he pushed a little more and asked how much. I didn't even hesitate. Without even thinking, I just said '$10,000.' I thought he would laugh. He didn't really react for a minute, and then he said he'd give me $5,000 on the spot. It was tempting, but I turned him down. That's pretty crazy, huh? He would have paid $5,000 for this old white rat."

Momma K had gotten herself busy in the kitchen by then, and

with a topic change as quick as a squirrel jumping from one tree branch to another, she said, "Have either of you heard from Levi or Isaac lately?"

Pops glanced at Coop and shrugged his shoulders.

She went on to say, "I have been talking to Annie recently. She is doing well. She's still goin' after the fashion world, her custom shirt designs are being received very well, and she has a big manufacturer looking at producing them. I think that is so exciting. Don't you?"

"I hadn't heard about the manufacturer. That is exciting!" Pops agreed.

Cooper also nodded in response, then spoke up, "You know the ranch I'm workin' on now, the Sun Light? Well they just bought a horse from Isaac, a big black half draft. They bought it for me to use because with all those big yearling cattle to rope and doctor, I needed a big, sturdy horse."

"Didn't Isaac call him Shaquille or something?" Momma K wondered.

"Yes he did," Cooper affirmed, "and I like him a lot. Anyway, when he delivered the horse to me, he stayed a day and we spent some good time together. He told me about all of the horses that he's training and how well the colt starting class that he is teaching at Montana State is going. So as far as I could tell, he's doing well, too."

"What about Levi?" she probed.

"Levi's pretty busy with all of the saddle orders that he has, but he's gonna start working on my new saddle soon. He has the tree already I just need to get him some more money so he can get the rest of the materials. Then I'll have a Hamely Daisy just like Levi, Isaac, and Pops have."

"I'll bet you're lookin' forward to that." Pops poked at him.

"Other than that, they're all doing well as far as I know."

As the conversation trailed off, Cooper said, "Well, I better get down the road. It's a long drive to Cody and I've got a lot to do once I get there." He packed what little things he had, loaded Gus into the truck, and he was off again, back to the ranch and livin' the dream.

A few weeks went by before he was heard from again. A Sunday afternoon phone call brought Pops and Momma K up to speed.

"Cooper, you must be missin' me. I'm glad you called. How are you and Gus doing?" Momma K was her usual happy self.

"That's what I'm callin' about," Coop said. There was deep frustration in his voice. "It's Gus, he's gone."

Before he could explain, she flooded him with concerns and questions. "Where is he? What happened? Did wolves from the park get him? Did someone take him? How can we help? Do you need us to come up there? You know we will."

After wading through the flood of questions with a series of yes and no answers, Coop filled her in on what had happened.

"I came into town to go to church," he said. "As usual, Gus was in the back of my pickup. I didn't want him to get bored and go exploring while I was inside, so I parked in a shady spot, hooked the chain in the truck bed to his collar, went into church, and didn't think another thing of it. When we came out, he was gone."

"Who is we?" Momma K asked.

"Oh, Clayton. He works with me at the ranch."

"What are you going to do now?"

"I'm goin' huntin' for him! Somebody had to have taken him—he was chained in and his collar is gone. I have no idea where to start, but I'll keep you posted."

Momma K asked, "Are you prayin'?"

"I sure am. Now I'd better go." He hung up and Momma K started to pray too, she prayed for Cooper and Gus, and for whoever took Gus that they might return him. She then filled Pops in on what was happening.

As Cooper sat in his truck deciding what to do next, he fiddled with his key chain and noticed his spurs draped around the base of the gear shift on the floor. His spurs, his Christmas spurs, the ones with the original rowels back in place, inspired by the matching spur rowels. He knew what he had to do.

First, he notified everyone he knew in the area about what had happened, knowing that timing was critical. With Clayton in tow, he methodically started to comb the town.

If a one-inch spur rowel could be found in a two thousand acre range pasture and Poppy could be recovered in a three state area, then surely a white, unusual-looking dog like Gus could be found in a mid-sized town in Wyoming. Couldn't he?

He started in the church parking lot. Could someone he knew there be playing a bad joke on him? He hoped it could be that simple. Nope. From there it was driving every street and searching.

As well as they could, at a slow drive by speed, they looked in every back yard and alley. He figured he better make a sweep of the entire area first, then if he had to, go back and look deeper.

After several hours of searching in a town of 10,000 people, they were running out of options. Cody is a place with all of the usual residential and commercial areas as any other town, but in addition to that, it is the destination at the northeast entrance of what is likely the most popular national park in the world. Yellowstone National Park with its tens of thousands of annual visitors, plus all of the tourist attractions that go along with a park such as bars, restaurants, motels, shops, and museums. Not to mention the popular nightly professional rodeo that's held at the fairgrounds that draws characters from all over. They venture in from Texas to Canada either to compete or just spectate. The thought of so many people passing through Cody, an almost continual stream of people during the summertime, was most concerning to Cooper. Gus could be put in the back of a car, motor home, or truck, and be many miles down the road in no time.

Toward the end of the day, they had covered most of the concentrated parts of town and were starting on the outskirts. Cooper decided to head out to the fairgrounds and have a look around. Near the grounds sat a large shopping center with many cars in the parking lot. Something told him to go look there. He drove up and down the stalls of cars, whistling and hollering Gus' name with his now hoarse voice. He was getting discouraged, but something from inside spurred him on. Surely Momma K's constant talking to the big ranch should provide some help, he thought.

All this time, Clayton had been patiently riding along. They were nearing the end of the lot with no luck yet. Coop continued to drive and call. Then at last, two rows of cars and trucks away, a dog with a white head popped up out of the back of a pick-up truck. Cooper could not drive there fast enough, neither for Gus or himself.

Cooper neared the truck and noticed that it had Texas plates. Nobody was in the truck, so he cut Gus loose. He had been tied to the back of the bed. Cooper was so relieved to see Gus and have him back, but now he was very bothered that he had obviously been stolen with no intentions of being returned. He thought, who does that? Who would steal a dog? Peering through the truck window, he could see Gus' collar with his own name and phone number plainly engraved on a steel plate attached to it. The truck was locked.

With mixed emotions of relief and anger, Cooper could not just take Gus and leave it at that. After putting Gus in the back seat of his own pickup and leaving Clayton to watch things, Coop marched into the store. From the service counter he asked for the owners of a certain pick-up from Texas to be paged. Then he went back to the truck. Soon after, three eighteen-year-old wannabe rodeo kids strolled out to see what was wanted.

Cooper was not really an intimidating figure. He didn't cast any more of a shadow than a skinny cedar post, albeit a long one. By now he was 21 years old and had grown to be 6'3". Luckily, he had on a bulky sweater, which gave him a little more of a presence. He had momentarily lost his usual charm and had turned on the rage of one who had been done wrong. The boys were getting a piece of his mind. He was sharing a host of "non-prayer words" with the boys, thumping one of them with his long finger and generally telling them where they could go and what they could do with Texas when they got there.

The store manager, who happened to be out picking up stray shopping carts, overheard the ruckus and attempted to intervene.

"Not to be disrespectful, Sir, but you had better just sit this one out," was Cooper's response. Coop had obviously seen too many John Wayne movies in his life and he was ready to take justice into his own hands and see to it that these rustlers got their due punishment.

The manager was a little taken aback by Cooper's boldness, but when he learned what the issue was, he understood where Coop was coming from. The boys were in town to ride rough stock in the nightly rodeo. The manager informed them that they were not welcome in the store anymore and told them to leave.

As Cooper, Clayton, and Gus started back to the ranch, Coop realized that he should have notified the authorities while Gus was tied in the truck and the collar was locked inside so it could all be proven. Could it be that he had John Wayned it a little too soon? Oh well, it was too late. He decided to do the next best thing.

He contacted the rodeo office and explained the whole situation. They recognized the boys by Coop's description and called them in. They were camped out near the arena in a fairly fancy living quarters horse trailer and a nice truck, obviously a rig owned by someone's daddy. They had all paid to ride in the nightly rodeo for a month, but they had only ridden a couple of nights. The rodeo committee disqualified them from riding, did not refund their entry fees, and escorted them out of town.

A little justice for rustling, Coop felt.

That evening, Momma K got another phone call. "Hello Coop. Tell me everything is all good," she held her breath and waited to hear.

"Oh we're fine. Now, anyway," he said dryly.

"You sound tired. Did you find Gus? Is he ok? Are you ok?"

"It's a long story that I haven't really processed yet."

He filled her in as best he could. He left out some details, just so she wouldn't worry. She got enough of the story to learn that it was a happy ending. Cooper and Gus were fine, back together, and ready to go back to work, like a pair of spurs with perfectly matching rowels.

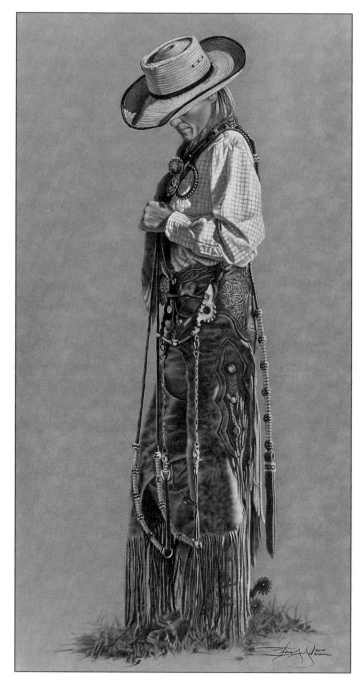

"Unbridled"

EPILOGUE

As Pops rides through the pasture checking on a little band of yearling cattle, he considers how well his young horse Pate is handling. They are some distance away from Momma K who is riding her favorite mare, Lady. Pate's not bothered in the least by the distance he is from his mother. His ears are attentive yet relaxed as he watches the cattle. For a young horse, his movements are soft and willing. Pops thinks to himself, boy, Isaac sure did a good job startin' this colt. I may just have to keep him for myself. They make a few small circles and he eases Pate up to wait for Momma K and Lady to catch up with them.

Pops' hands slide to adjust the bubble in his mecate, the braid is smooth and colorful, a piece of work to brag on for sure. Coop has come a long way in perfecting this craft of braiding. How many of these has he braided? Pops wonders.

Coming to a complete stop, he feels nothing in the shape of the saddle seat, as it should be with quality craftsmanship. Pops' custom "Hamley Daisy" is sure enough quality. As he settles to wait, his fingers unconsciously linger on the maker stamp carved deep in the front of the seat leather. He traces the letters, "Levi Johnson— Maker." Pops couldn't be more proud sitting Tall in this Saddle, one that fits just right.

Even from the distance she now lives, away from the thousand acres of river bottoms and her guys, Cheyenne keeps ol' Pops wrangled in, or at least she keeps him in Wranglers. She is a traveling rep for the clothing company.

Moments later, Momma K sidles up alongside Pops and catches him in his far off reminiscing. "Watcha' thinkin' about?" she asks.

Pops looks at her and says, "Oh, I was just thinkin', you know, life sure is good."

"Is that all?"

He thoughtfully considers and says, "Well, along with that, I was also realizing that even the very worst day in the saddle is better than the best day anywhere else. What do you think?"

She smiles and nods in agreement.

TALL IN THE SADDLE

Come share this crazy fun-filled adventure,
Hang tight for the ride where e're it goes;
Over peaks, through valleys and pasture,
From deserts to belly-deep snows.

Hear the squeak of well-worn saddles,
Cherish good times for kids of all ages,
Peek into the past and glimpse the future,
Stir memories with the turn of these pages.

Cherished images will fill your mind
Like scenes from an old time picture show.
The vast blue sky was his limit then,
There was not a place that he couldn't go.

Life was lived at a fun easy pace,
In all his boyhood reflection.
Many good times were there to be had,
With a pony to make the connection.

Soaring with eagles, scouting the prairie,
Finding where buffalo roam.
Racing for the gold cup at a fan-filled track,
Or fresh baked cookies at home.

When backyards were barnyards,
Hay barns turned into kids' huts,
Fenced fields for baseball, ditches for swimming,
And driveways were two muddy ruts.

The Fourth of July was picnics and fireworks,
Rodeos, games and small country fairs,
Where friends and relatives coming from town
Would escape from their everyday cares.

Parades had bicycles, horses and wagons,
And floats with people well-known.
But out on the farm on the road by the barn,
We'd have a parade of our own.

Looking back he could do all this and more,
Through all his boyhood reflection,
With his old dog Belle, a stick for a sword,
And again, a pony to make the connection.

Cake and ice cream couldn't compete
With his pony hitched to the cart.
Kids lined up for a turn on the seat,
And giggles came straight from the heart.

His pony and he would be a mighty fine sight,
In a WILD WEST Bill Cody show.
He'd save a fair maiden from the black knight,
While slayin' dragons in the full moon's glow.

Lay back in the grass on the bank of a brook,
Where dreams and reality tend to collide.
See drifting cloud ponies, and a fish on the hook,
Think of the "Dandy" he was priviledged to ride.

When it's all said and done,
No matter your age or your size,
If you want a life full of fun,
Then here's a word to the wise.

If you're too short with your feet on the ground,
Then find a good pony to straddle.
This cowboy fact is easily found,
You're never so tall as when you sit in the saddle.